IN A LOWLY PLACE

The Reed Ferguson Mystery Series, Book 21

RENÉE PAWLISH

A Reed Ferguson Mystery

First Digital Edition published by Creative Cat Press
copyright 2022 by Renée Pawlish

ACKNOWLEDGMENTS

The author gratefully acknowledges all those who helped in the writing of this book, including: Beth Treat and Beth Higgins. A special thanks to Marlen Van Matre and Jatonya Turner for their help with cancer research. Any mistakes with that are mine. If I've forgotten anyone, please accept my apologies.

To all my beta readers: I am in your debt!

Sheree Benson, Dianne Biscoe, Van Brollini, Gerry Draper, Betty Jo English, Tracy Gestewitz, Maxine Lauer, Becky Neilsen, Fritzi Redgrave, Albert Stevens, Joyce Stumpff, Marlene Van Matre, Barry Weisbord

CHAPTER ONE

"Where is he?" Michelle Farley looked around the Starbucks, then her gaze settled back on me. She picked up her latte, took a sip, and put the cup down with a small shrug. "I told him four o'clock."

It was a gloomy August afternoon, the earlier heat of the day yielding to threatening storms in the west. We were sitting outside the Starbucks on Sixteenth and Arapahoe, a place I – Reed Ferguson, private eye extraordinaire – often choose to meet potential clients. Michelle had called me the previous day to say that she'd wanted to hire me to help her brother, Dennis Mowery. She hadn't said what was going on, but that she and her brother would meet me here today. I watched people approach the Starbucks as we talked.

"I can't believe I'm talking to a private investigator," Michelle said. She appeared to be in her late forties, with shoulder-length pale blond hair and a thin face. I was drawn to her hazel eyes – same color as mine. She was petite and looked small sitting in the chair. I waited and she went on. "You probably think I'm crazy."

"Not at all." I leaned forward and smiled. "What's going on?"

"Look for a guy with curly dark hair and a goatee." She looked up and down the mall and scowled. Then she finally said, "I want your help with Dennis."

"For?"

She bit her lip. "Dennis is my younger brother, by three years. Then there's our brother, Isaac. He's two years younger than Dennis. We all work at a trucking company – Mowery Transportation – that our father started. Scratch that, Isaac and I work there. Dennis used to work with us, but not anymore."

I took a sip of my macchiato. "Why not?"

She let out a sigh that held a lot of angst in it. "That's why I'm coming to you." She thought for a second. "Let me back up. Everything seemed to be going fine with all of us, and with the business, until about three years ago. Believe it or not, the trucking business isn't as straightforward as you might assume. It can be tricky. There are affiliate agreements with trucking companies, and there's lots of competition, but we've worked with some great partners. But things changed, and it affected our business. It took some time to get things running smoothly again. About that time, Dennis went off the deep end." A quick breeze wafted her perfume in my direction. She touched at her hair. "Dennis was our accountant and oversaw finances. I handle the scheduling department, and Isaac manages the in-house diesel technicians and the big rigs. Our father's in charge of the whole operation. Anyway, as we hit that rough patch, something happened with Dennis. He had always been a happy guy. Nothing seemed to bother him. But then he changed. He was edgy a lot, and he would snap at you. The family used to see him a lot after work and on the weekends, but that stopped. I didn't understand the change in behavior."

"I'm assuming you asked him about it?"

She nodded. "Yes, of course. He would either deny that anything was wrong, or he'd say there was something going on at home. But that didn't seem plausible."

"What didn't seem plausible? Either of those, or both?"

"Both. Dennis was never in any trouble, even as a teenager. He kept to the straight and narrow, went to college in Florida, worked at an accounting firm for a while so that he felt he knew the ropes before he came to work at Dad's trucking company. And at least at the beginning, there weren't any problems with his wife, Kim. I know her pretty well, and we've gotten along over the years. I asked her several times about Dennis's strange behavior, and she said things were okay."

In my time as an investigator, I've learned not to trust everything I hear. I knew that just because she thought things were okay with her brother didn't mean that was the case. Even as the words were coming out of her mouth, I knew that if I took this case, I would need to talk to Kim herself to get her take on her relationship with Dennis.

"What did your brother Isaac think about Dennis?" I asked.

She looked to the mall again, searching for Dennis, then took a drink. "Isaac was as mystified as I was. He told me he tried to talk to Dennis, but Dennis wouldn't talk to him. You should talk to Isaac to see what he thinks."

I knew I would do that as well – again, if I took the case. "You mentioned some problems at the company. Would any of that factor into Dennis's change of behavior?"

"I don't know. We managed to get through the tough times, get things back on track. I know there was some stress for Dennis. There usually is when you're working for a family business, and when the finances were strained, that got to him. But we all told him it wasn't his fault. I wouldn't have thought that the financial problems would've sent him over the edge."

"What changes did you see in Dennis?"

"He began drinking heavily, which was already unusual, because he was never much of a drinker. He couldn't control it. It all happened very fast, and after about a year of his erratic behavior, Kim threw him out. Dennis seemed to be a lost cause. At first, he lived in a motel, and he wasn't reliable at work, was making mistakes. Kim couldn't take it anymore, and she filed for divorce." She frowned. "I wish she'd have given it a little more time, but I don't blame her. At that point, Dennis had nothing, and he was living in his car. Dad finally couldn't take the crazy behavior, and he fired Dennis. Then we lost touch with Dennis for about a year. I had no idea where he was or what he was doing. Then, just like that," she snapped her fingers, "a few months ago, he called me out of the blue. He told me he was clean and sober, and that he was living at Step Recovery. It's a halfway house here in Denver for hard-core street people to get back on their feet. He apologized for everything he'd done and said he wanted to try to make things right."

"Sorry for the drinking?" I wondered if there was more that Dennis needed to apologize for, that she wasn't saying.

She nodded. "The drinking, and for disappearing without a word. When he disappeared, we were all devastated and worried sick. I couldn't believe he called, and we got together for lunch. It was so great to see him, to know that he was alive." Her eyes crinkled sadly. "He'd changed, though, and physically he didn't look that great. It broke my heart to see him like that, but I was just so relieved, I didn't care what he looked like. We've been talking since then. He's been a bit distant, like he's embarrassed. I've only seen him a handful of times."

"What had he been doing the whole time he was out of touch?"

"He'd been living in his car, and even at times, he wouldn't know where his car was and he'd be on the streets. I asked him how he paid for things, and he said he sold his car, then worked odd jobs and begged for money." Her tone was a mix of grief and embarrassment. "It was sad to think he'd sunk so low. Then he said that one morning he woke up under a bridge lying in his own vomit, and something snapped in him, and he realized he didn't want to live like that anymore. He knew a guy who was at Step Recovery, and Dennis went there. He worked hard to clean himself up, and he's working on staying sober. I told him that we would be there to help him, that we could consider having him work at the company again, if he stays clean. For now, he says that's not what he wants. He needs to know that he can stay clean and sober before he thinks about working for Mowery Transportation again."

There was something about what she said that didn't quite sit right with me. I could understand the embarrassment Dennis must've felt, but was that enough to keep him from jumping at the chance for a better job, a better position?

"Do Dennis and Kim have any kids?"

She shook her head. "No, they don't. They had trouble conceiving, and I think they were considering adoption, but then all this started happening with Dennis and they didn't."

"You and Isaac got along with Dennis?"

"I do. Isaac and Dennis generally got along, although they fought sometimes. They're different personalities. Dennis is quiet and reserved. Isaac is outgoing and he can be brash."

I again got the feeling there was more than she was telling me. I glanced up and down the mall. It was fifteen minutes after Dennis was supposed to meet us. He was clearly a no-show. I looked at Michelle.

"What is it exactly that you want me to do?"

She pursed her lips. "As I said before, this may sound crazy, but I was hoping you would befriend Dennis, talk to him. Something happened a few years ago that sent him on this path. When we've talked recently, I've asked him about it, and he won't tell me. Call it a sister's intuition, but I'm certain something happened that made him start drinking and lose control of his life. I pushed him about it, but he's just so evasive. He keeps telling me that the past is the past, and he needs to move forward. But even I know how AA works, how you have your twelve steps, and how you need to make amends to people. He's been doing some of that, reaching out to people to apologize. But there's something more there, and I'm worried that if it isn't resolved, Dennis may start drinking again. I figured if he wouldn't talk to me, maybe he would tell you."

I thought about that for a moment. "Don't you think that's a stretch? Why would he tell a stranger what he wouldn't tell you?"

"Yes, it may be. But if he won't talk to you, can you do some poking around, see if you can find out what happened?"

I finished my macchiato while I mulled over her proposal. My best friend, Cal Whitmore, always addresses me as "Great Detective." But at the moment, I wasn't feeling very "great," certainly not "in demand." I'd just wrapped up a case for a small insurance company where I'd investigated a false injury claim. It had been an easy job, and it certainly didn't skirt any greatness. I could use the work, that was for sure. But what Michelle proposed didn't sound like the type of thing I could help with, and I told her so. "I'm sorry, but if Dennis isn't going to talk to his own family – which I get that he might not want to – I don't see how he'd want to talk to me, either."

She blinked at me, disappointment passing across her face. Then she dabbed at her eyes. "I guess I see your point, and maybe it was silly of me to even think this might work. I so badly want Dennis to succeed, to get back on his feet. I don't want to see anything threaten his sobriety. If he starts drinking again, I don't know if my parents could take it. They love us all, but they dote on Dennis. They couldn't believe it when he started drinking like he did, and that his life would get so out of control. They've been ecstatic to see him again, even though he doesn't look that great. They have their estranged son back." She took her cup, started to take a drink, then set it down with disinterest. She locked eyes with me. "There's no way I could change your mind?"

I thought for a moment and shook my head. "I'm sorry, but I think it would be a waste of time." I looked at the people hustling about the mall. "Maybe if I'd had a chance to talk to Dennis, but he didn't show up. It doesn't seem like he wanted to talk to you or me today. I think that tells us what we need to know."

"Yes, I think you're right." She was suddenly very matter-of-fact. She pushed back from the table and stood up. "I'm sorry I wasted your time." She spilled her latte on the table as she snatched up her cup. She gave me a quick smile, threw the cup in a trash can, and whirled around and walked onto the mall. I waited until she disappeared in the crowd, then grabbed a napkin and wiped the table.

CHAPTER TWO

Apparently, I wasn't going to find out any more about Dennis Mowery. I got up and threw my cup in the trash can with disgust. The wind picked up and blew a piece of paper down the Sixteenth Street Mall. I felt like that piece of paper: aimless. I glanced up at the clouds, and they seemed darker than before. I'd have to hurry to my car and hope that I didn't get rained on. I headed toward Champa Street. The mall was crowded, even with the storm threatening. It was almost 4:30. Business people were heading home, tourists popped in and out of shops, and the outdoor seating at several restaurants was packed. I crossed Champa and then suddenly stopped at the other corner. Up ahead, a man in a wrinkled brown suit was peering in a store window. He had curly black hair and a goatee, just as Michelle had described her brother.

Dennis Mowery?

I watched him for a moment. He was tall with broad shoulders and thin enough that the suit hung loosely on his frame. I puzzled as he continued to look in the window. Michelle and I had waited twenty minutes past the time we'd agreed to meet at the Starbucks. I assumed the man was Dennis, so why wasn't he headed to the coffee shop now?

The man started in the other direction, and I followed. He seemed oblivious to my presence, so I called out "Dennis!" He glanced over his shoulder, saw me, and began trotting away.

"Hey!" I said as I picked up my pace.

I was sure it was Dennis. He dodged around a few people, crossed Stout Street, and hurried down the mall, then turned the corner. I raced after him, irritated, and curious. Why run from me? I stepped past some teenagers who were loitering in front of the TJ Maxx store and rounded the corner of the building. Then a fist glanced off the side of my face.

"Ow!" I snarled. I looked up to see Dennis standing there, a fist still raised. "What did you do that for?" I asked as I put a hand to my cheek.

"You okay?" a man who was standing near the corner asked.

"Yeah, I'm fine," I muttered.

My cheek smarted, and my ire was up. But I'd live. A few people walked past, and no one on the mall paid attention to us. A flash of lightning split the sky as I studied Dennis. Up close, he wasn't quite what I'd expected. Michelle had said he didn't look great, but that missed the mark. He face was gaunt, with drawn cheeks as worn and frazzled as his clothes. Wrinkles etched his brow, and his hollow eyes were full of caution. Up close, I could see that his suit wasn't just wrinkled, but threadbare.

"You're Dennis Mowery?" I snapped.

He hesitated. "Yes."

"Want to put that fist down? Or are we going to duke it out right here?" I hadn't been in a fistfight since high school, but I was mad enough at the moment to take him on. He slowly lowered his hand, but wariness danced in his eyes. "Why'd you run away from me?" I asked.

He shrugged. "I don't know. I guess I was having second thoughts about meeting you and my sister. I was debating what to do when you called my name. I panicked. It didn't help that you came after me." Now he was the one who sounded irritated. "The last year or so I've had to watch over my shoulder a lot." Another shrug. "I guess old habits die hard."

A rumble of thunder punctuated his words. He stared at me, then glanced over my shoulder.

"Your sister left," I said.

"Oh."

"So do you want to talk to me or not?" We were off to a bad start, and I tried to keep the annoyance at bay. It wasn't working.

He shifted from foot to foot. "I'm sorry I didn't show up at Starbucks. I'm not sure what I should do."

His gaze darted to the mall again. I looked in that direction, but didn't see anything unusual. I gestured toward a bench on the mall.

"Want to tell me about it?" I asked.

He glanced up at the dark sky and said, "I guess so. At least until it rains on us."

We moved over to the bench and sat down. A mall shuttle bus drove past, and Dennis waited. Then he ran a hand over his pants.

"What'd my sister tell you about me?"

"That you've had a rough few years." I gave him the condensed version of what Michelle had said.

He rubbed a hand slowly over his chin and nodded thoughtfully. "She doesn't know the half of it."

"Want to enlighten me?"

He shifted and rested an arm on the back of the bench, then locked eyes with me. "There are a lot of reasons why I started drinking, but things got really bad when someone started blackmailing me."

"Really?"

He nodded, and I waited him out. He fidgeted with some chipped paint on the bench, then finally went on. "I guess I should back up. As I said, the last few years have been tough. I was actually homeless until recently. Now I'm at a halfway house, clean and sober." He let out a little laugh. "Hard to believe that at one point in time, I was dining at the Chophouse or Shanahan's Steakhouse. Nice cars, vacations. I was doing really well." He looked down the mall again, then pulled at the lapels of his shabby suit. "I dressed up for today, but can you believe this suit? I shouldn't complain; someone donated the clothes. But I used to have nice clothes. I didn't get any of them in the divorce, and they wouldn't fit now anyway."

"What happened?"

He turned back to me. "I got cocky and stupid. I worked at the family company, which was fine. Things were going along great, and then I hurt my knee. They prescribed OxyContin for me, and I got hooked on it. Do you know how much it can cost to keep up an addiction like that?"

I shook my head. "I know it's enough to ruin people."

He snorted. "Yeah, that's true. I would spend way more than I was making, trying to keep up with the bills, and trying to keep up with my addiction. And I was drinking, too." He stared at the ground for a moment. "Things grew out of control. I lost my marriage and my job." He sucked in a breath. "My wife kicked me out, and I stayed in a motel. I had nothing, and when we divorced, she was the one who still had the job, so she got the house. I never thought I'd end up living in my car, but that's exactly what happened."

I looked at him, and his eyes darted away. Something about his story didn't quite add up.

"There's something you're not telling me," I said.

He nodded slowly. "It wasn't just the drugs and drinking." He looked down almost as if in shame. "Michelle doesn't know this, but I started skimming money from the company, a little bit here, little bit there. I could change things in contracts, adjust financials. Small enough that no one would notice, unless they were looking carefully. And no one did. I justified it by saying that no one would know, that the company would do just fine without the money, that kind of thing. Then it grew to more money, but I was still able to cover it up." He stared at the ground. "One day it all came crashing down. Someone – I have no idea who it was – figured it out, and they started blackmailing me. I received a note at work saying that if I didn't pay ten thousand dollars, they'd tell my dad and the rest of the family about it."

Now I was intrigued. "And you paid it?"

"Of course I paid it." A couple of small raindrops fell, but he didn't notice. I wasn't going to say anything that might stop him from talking. "I couldn't afford to get caught. But the only way for me to come up with that kind of money was to keep skimming." He scowled. "Hell, what a position for me to be in. The drinking and drugs kept me going and kept me from feeling the guilt about what I was doing, and I needed money for the booze and drugs. It might've been fine if it had stopped at that, but then the blackmailer wanted more. And I had to continue to steal to pay off whoever this was. The hole just got deeper and deeper. I ended up paying three separate times, a total of fifty grand. I was so worried I'd get caught, and so worried the blackmailer would keep asking for more."

His face fell, and I felt sorry for him.

"You're sure Michelle doesn't know? Or Isaac or your dad?" I asked. "She mentioned you were making mistakes at work."

"They would've confronted me about it. It wasn't that obvious. I was the accountant, and I knew how to hide what I was doing."

Or one of them was blackmailing you and didn't want your skimming to stop. "And then what?"

"I lost my marriage and then my job. I ended up on the street, drinking and drugging, mostly in a haze." A little sniff. "I could never have imagined myself in that position. The blackmailing stopped. At least I think it did. No one knew how to get hold of me, and I didn't have a job. Where would I get the money to pay off anyone?" He laughed without humor. "But a few months ago, something changed for me. I got tired of living like I was living, and I knew I needed to do something. I've been in and out of enough homeless shelters to know there was help, if I wanted it, and so I started making changes. I'm clean and sober. It hasn't been easy, and I haven't been able to get steady work, but I'm trying. I've been working a 12-step program, trying to make amends for the things I've done wrong." He lapsed into silence.

"Your sister thinks that if you don't address what happened in the past, you might start drinking again."

He gave that some thought. "It bothers me, not knowing who blackmailed me. I don't want to get revenge on them or anything like that, I just want to know. That's been eating at me this whole time."

The rain started a little harder, and I gestured toward California Street. "My car's down there. We can talk more there, if you want."

He nodded and we got up. He seemed nervous as we hurried down California.

"You have no idea who was blackmailing you?" I asked as we headed toward my 4-Runner.

"No, I don't." He ran a hand through his hair. "I suppose it could have been somebody at the company, but it's just as possible it was someone else."

"Really? Who else could've found out about your stealing from the company?"

He swore. "I don't know. It's not like I advertised what I'd been doing."

The rain came down harder as we reached my car. I unlocked it, and we got in. I peered out the windshield. People were scrambling to find shelter.

"If I take the case, and if I find your blackmailer, what're you going to do with that information?" I asked.

He sighed. "I don't know that I'll do anything. I just want to know who it was."

"I don't want anything to do with a revenge scenario."

"It's not about that. That won't help my sobriety."

He seemed sincere in that, but I knew I needed to proceed cautiously. "Your family should know what you did."

He eyed me. "It needs to come from me."

"I won't say anything."

I studied him for a moment as the rain pattered down on the roof of the SUV. I respected somebody who was trying to turn his life around. He didn't look as if he could afford much, and I found myself sympathizing with him. Except for when he punched me.

"Your sister's willing to pay me to help you," I said. "You'd be okay with that?"

He nodded. "I'll pay her back somehow."

If Dennis was willing to work with me – and it seemed he was – this changed things. I decided to take the case, and I told him so. Then we got down to business.

CHAPTER THREE

The rain continued to pound my car. Dennis stared out the windshield, his face forlorn. I did feel sorry for the guy.

"Can I drive you somewhere?" I asked.

"If you don't mind. I'd sure hate to be waiting for a bus in the middle of this." He glanced upward. "Who knows how long it'll rain."

"You don't have your car?"

He shrugged. "I sold it a while ago. I needed the money." He smiled halfheartedly. "Can you imagine living in a car, though?"

I shook my head and started the 4-Runner. "Where to?"

"Twentieth and Larimer. A place called Step Recovery. It's a shelter and halfway-house started by a drunk." He drew in a breath and let it out slowly. "It's not a bad place, although sometimes I don't feel like I fit in. Some of the guys there have been on the street for a long time. Their stories aren't quite like mine." He lifted a hand to dismiss that thought. "Although, I guess I shouldn't be talking. I've made a mess of my life."

I didn't respond as I glanced over my shoulder and pulled into the street. As I stopped at a light, I said, "If I'm going to find who blackmailed you, I'll need to talk to your family, your ex-wife, friends, that kind of thing. Are you okay with that?"

His answer took a long time. "I guess so. You'll have to tell them about me skimming money from the company?"

"I don't see how I can keep that a secret."

He nodded. "Yeah, I see your point. But why don't you let me tell Michelle and Isaac. And my dad. I want them to hear it from me, not you. When I get back to the shelter, I'll call Michelle and tell her you changed your mind, that you're going to help. Maybe she can get a payment to you, as well."

The light changed and I pressed the gas. "Okay. I should talk to her again, but I'll wait until tomorrow." He didn't say anything to that, and I went on. "What about your ex?"

"What about her?" The tone rose, then quickly crashed. "Oh, about skimming the money, and the blackmail. That's fine if you talk to her. I doubt she'll care now."

"Have you tried to contact her since you sobered up?"

He shook his head. "She wouldn't want that. Remember, she threw me out. She was really steamed about everything I'd done."

"Did she know you were being blackmailed?"

"No ..." He hesitated.

"What?" I asked.

"I said a lot of things when I was drunk or high. I suppose I could've mentioned being blackmailed, but she never said anything about it."

"My guess would be if she knew, she'd have told you and possibly other people, including your family."

"True."

"Has she remarried?"

He shook his head. "Not that I'm aware of."

There was something in his voice – regret, I suppose – but something else I couldn't quite put my finger on. We drove in silence for a moment.

"Was your marriage good before you got into such a bad place?" I asked.

He took a moment before he answered. "Yeah, it was fine. We had our ups and downs, the occasional fight, but overall it was okay."

"Even after your drinking and drug use started?"

He grimaced. "That didn't interfere with things for quite a while. I was able to hide it well. It was only near the end that things went to hell. At that point, I was in a fog most of the time."

"You weren't in any other trouble?"

"No."

"How do you fill your days now?" I asked as I followed traffic onto Larimer Street.

He bit his lip. "Day labor for the moment. Part of living at Step Recovery is getting full-time work. I'm working with a career counselor now, trying to find a good fit. I was never that handy, but I've learned. Most of what I can get now is construction work. It's okay, but I'd like to get back into some other work. But with my history ..." He glanced in the side mirror.

"You don't have kids, correct?"

He shook his head. "No, we tried, but it never happened. It's probably a good thing, given how things turned out."

"So no way that Kim was somehow involved in the blackmail? Maybe you slipped and talked about skimming from the company and she blackmailed you?"

"That sounds a little farfetched."

"Maybe. I've seen stranger things."

"We had plenty of money, and she made good money herself."

"What does she do?"

"She's an architect. Still is, as far as I know. Her firm works on commercial projects. She makes great money."

"What firm?"

"Rockridge Architecture."

I crossed Twentieth and found a parking place in front of a small bar, then looked across the street. Step Recovery was in a long two-story brick building a stone's throw from Coors Field, where the Colorado Rockies baseball team plays. Next door to Step was the Marquis Theater, a venue for small concerts, and on the other side of Step was a little parking lot enclosed by an iron fence. By now, the rain had stopped, but puddles remained.

"Tell me about the last days before you lost your job."

A dark cloud passed across his face. "Kim was furious most of the time. I was barely functioning with the drug use. She finally told me she'd had enough. We had an incredible fight one night; I still remember it. It was snowing outside, so beautiful, and yet we were screaming and yelling at each other. I guess we were lucky it wasn't summertime with the windows open, or the neighbors would've been treated to quite a show. She threw a coffee cup at me and told me to get out. I was so naïve. I thought it would just be something temporary, but it wasn't. I never went back in the house."

"You didn't get any of your belongings?"

Of all the things he'd said, that really struck me. I instantly pictured what I'd lose if I had to leave home with no chance to take anything at all with me. I knew what would be the greatest loss, materially speaking at least: I'm a film noir buff, love the old movies with the noir hero and the femme fatales. I have a huge DVD collection, as well as a very respectable collection of first-edition detective novels. My prizes are first editions of *A Study in Scarlet*, by Sir Arthur Conan Doyle, and Raymond Chandler's *The Long Goodbye*. I keep those in a glass case in my home office. God forbid, my sweet wife, Willie, ever kicked me out. But if she did, I'd want to retrieve those things. Thankfully, I didn't see that happening.

"No, I didn't," he replied.

I turned to look at Dennis. He reminded me a bit of those noir heroes, not because he'd committed a crime but because he was down on his luck. I even wondered whether his ex, Kim, was a femme fatale, a seductress tempting the noir hero into compromising situations. But then, I snapped out of my film noir reverie and returned to the situation at hand. I knew I needed to talk to Kim, and when I did, I'd see if she fit the femme fatale role.

"What else do you want to know?" Dennis asked.

I took out my phone, opened a notes app, and typed in Kim's workplace. "Besides your family, who else at the company should I talk to?"

"Why?" His tone bordered on defensive.

"Some of them might know who was blackmailing you."

"I guess so." He turned red. "I'm not sure I want to hear what they think of me after everything that happened." I looked at him expectantly, and he continued. "I don't know who you should talk to. I wasn't that close to anybody. I also don't know who still works there and who's left."

"I'll see what I can find out."

He glanced around, then checked the side mirror again.

"Are you worried about something?" I asked.

"No." A quick reply.

I checked the rearview mirror and saw cars passing by and two men crossing the street. Dennis seemed tense. I thought for a moment. "You really have no idea who might have been blackmailing you? Any friends I should talk to?"

He shook his head again. "I really don't. I tried to figure it out, tried to watch my back, but I never did know who was on to me. How does this work? Will you give me an update?"

I nodded. "Do you have a cell phone?"

"Just a temporary one."

He gave me the number, and I put it into my phone. "Okay. Give me a day or two to do some digging, and I'll let you know how things are going."

He thanked me and opened the car door. "I hope you have better luck finding this guy than I did."

I wasn't sure what the sudden rush to leave was about. "Hold on. You said you received a note from the blackmailer."

He stopped with one leg out of the car. "Yes. It came to the office. Thankfully no one opened my mail. It didn't have a return address."

"Do you still have the note?"

"No. I burned it, but I remember it said, 'We know you're stealing from the company.' I was to call a number at a certain time and I would receive instructions. So I did."

"You didn't recognize the number?"

"No."

"Was the note handwritten or printed?"

"Printed. Same with the envelope. There wasn't anything distinguishing about either that might've helped me figure out who sent it."

"So you called the number and ..."

"The person's voice was disguised, like one of those electronic voices you hear about in movies, so I didn't even know if it was a man or woman, or whether he or she had an accent. Nothing."

"What were you told to do?" I asked.

"Well," he said and then explained.

CHAPTER FOUR

Billy's on Broadway is a restaurant on, you guessed it, Broadway, a few miles south of downtown. I sat at a booth in the corner, sipped water, and watched what was going on. Dennis had told me that this was where he had passed off the blackmail money. I'd asked Willie to meet me there since it was almost dinnertime. Willie – given name Willimena – is an admissions nurse in the ER at Saint Joseph's Hospital, and her shift had just ended. I was thinking about her when a waitress came up to the table. I smiled at her.

"Welcome to Billy's. May I get you something to drink?"

"I'll have a Coke for now." I gestured to the empty seat across from me. "My wife will be joining me soon, and then we'll order." I held up the menu. "What's good here?"

"Oh, we're famous for our gourmet hot dogs, but if you're not in the mood for that, we have excellent coal-fired pizza."

I smiled back. "Okay, I'll keep that in mind."

"Let me get your drink."

She turned on her heel and walked away. She was young, probably no more than twenty-one or twenty-two, with long brown hair that framed a cute face. Perky. I looked around. It was getting busy, tables filling up, a din of conversation. Dennis hadn't known much about the restaurant, so I now looked it up online. Billy's was a family-owned place that had been in business for over sixty years, located in the same historic building. The waitress came back to the table, and I tried to pour on the charm.

"Hey, Jenny," I said, noting her name badge. "How long have you been working here?"

"A few years now," she said as she placed a Coke in front of me. "My parents own the place, and I've been working here since high school. I'll be headed back to college soon."

"Where?"

"Wyoming. We have relatives up there."

I led into my next question. "If you've been here a while, you might remember a waiter that worked here a little over a year ago. Taylor?" I gave her the name Dennis had given me. "I don't know his last name."

"That would have been Taylor Walsh. He doesn't work here anymore."

I frowned. "When did he leave?"

She shrugged. "I don't remember. It's been a while now."

"Six months? Eight months?" I pressed.

Her attention strayed to a nearby table. "I don't really remember."

"Do you know what job he took when he left here?"

"What are all these questions about?" She eyed me carefully.

I tried the charm again. "I need to track him down. It's important."

"I wish I could help you, but I can't. Do you want to order anything now, an appetizer, or wait for your wife?"

"I'll wait."

She smiled hesitantly as she took a couple of steps back and then walked away. I quickly googled Taylor Walsh. There were several in the Denver metro area. Which was the correct one? Without more information, I could spend days looking for him.

I picked up my Coke and took a drink, then thought about what else Dennis had told me. The exchange to pay off the blackmailer had been simple. Dennis was instructed to come to Billy's and sit at the booth near the door, where I was sitting now. A man named Taylor would wait on him, and during the meal, Dennis was supposed to tell Taylor he had a delivery. Ten thousand dollars to be exact, although he didn't tell Taylor that. Dennis had the money in an envelope that he was supposed to put on the table, and sometime during the meal, Taylor would take the envelope. Dennis had been specifically instructed not to leave the table until he finished his meal, and definitely not when Taylor took the envelope.

I studied the layout of the restaurant. There were only a few places that Taylor could have gone once he picked up the envelope. First would've been out the front door, but Dennis said that hadn't happened. The second was down a hallway. I could see doors to restrooms, and one to the kitchen. The first time Dennis had paid the blackmailer, Taylor had initially gone into the kitchen, but the second time, Taylor had gone down the hall to the restrooms for a minute. Then he'd reappeared before going into the kitchen. Dennis wasn't sure what Taylor had done with the envelope because Dennis did what he'd been instructed to do, and he remained at the table. As I'd heard the story from Dennis, I concluded a couple of things. First, I had to figure out whether Taylor was the blackmailer. Dennis didn't know him, but it was possible Taylor somehow knew Dennis, and knew about his skimming from the company. However, if that was the case, why would Taylor allow Dennis to know his real name? Second, if Taylor wasn't the blackmailer, would the blackmailer have stayed around, either in the restaurant or outside watching through a window to make sure that Dennis remained where he was, and that Taylor picked up the money but didn't keep it himself?

As I sat and waited, Jenny avoided my table. She didn't want to deal with my questions. Fair enough. I got up and went to the restroom to wash my hands and noticed another door at the end of the hall. Probably an office. When I returned to my booth, I went back over the blackmail scenario. It seemed likely that, if Taylor had been just the go-between, the blackmailer could trust him. Otherwise it was possible that Taylor could take all or part of the money instead of delivering it to the blackmailer. I was trying to remember what Dennis had told me about the last time he'd paid the blackmail money. Then Willie walked in and interrupted my thoughts. She was still in her purple hospital scrubs. I never tire of seeing her in those. Who knew scrubs could be so attractive? She leaned over and gave me a kiss, then slid into the seat across from me.

"Whew, what a day," she said as she ran a hand through her shoulder-length blond hair. "It was busier than normal." Then she gave me a little smile. "How was your day?" She looked around. "This is an interesting choice. We've never been here before."

"I'm on a new case." I slid the menu to her and told her what had transpired that afternoon.

"That sounds interesting," she said. She perused the menu. "What's good here?"

"I'm told the gourmet hot dogs."

Her face pinched. "Gourmet hot dogs? I'm not in the mood for that. I think I'll have the Mediterranean pizza."

I nodded. "Good choice. I'm going to try the monster dog."

Jenny returned and smiled at Willie, but avoided eye contact with me. She took our orders, and I tried again to get her to talk about Taylor Walsh. Jenny glanced at Willie, then quickly moved away. I gave Willie a few more details about my new case, and then she put her hand over mine.

"How are you going to track down this blackmailer, if Taylor doesn't work here anymore?"

"That's a good question." I watched as Jenny went to another table and chatted for a moment, then disappeared into the kitchen. "I think I scared her away."

"Did you tell her you're a PI?" Willie asked.

I shook my head. "I thought she'd clam up, not tell me anything."

"That didn't work," she observed wryly.

"I really need to track down Taylor Walsh."

Jenny came out of the kitchen and stood for a moment next to a long bar.

"Hold on," Willie said.

She got up and walked over to Jenny, spoke to her, and came back. She sat down and sighed.

"No luck," Willie said.

"What did you ask her?"

"I said my husband is a stalker and he needs to know where Taylor

Walsh is." A smile spread across her face. "Obviously, she didn't want to tell me anything."

"Some detective you are," I said.

She laughed. "Hey, I try. Actually, I forgot to order a drink, so I told her what I wanted."

I rolled my eyes as Willie laughed. Jenny brought Willie a glass of wine, then a few minutes later she returned with our meals. By then I'd decided I needed to be tactful but forceful. As Jenny put our plates down, I pulled out my wallet and showed her my private investigator's license.

"I hate to keep asking you about Taylor, but it's important. I need to track him down."

Jenny's face took on a hint of alarm, but she remained cool. "I really shouldn't tell you about Taylor. You know, privacy and all."

"Do you know where Taylor lives?" I asked.

Jenny shook her head. "I didn't know him very well. He worked here for a number of years, but I mostly saw him in passing. We tended to be on different shifts, because I was working around my school schedule."

"You said your parents own the restaurant?"

She nodded and glanced at Willie. Willie took a bite of her pizza, but gave Jenny an encouraging smile.

"Yes, they do," Jenny said

"Could I talk to one of them?" I asked. "That takes you off the hook."

Relief washed over her. "My dad's in the office now. I'll go get him."

She hurried away, and I bit into my hot dog. "I wonder what she'll tell her dad."

"I'm sure she's thinking Taylor is in some kind of trouble."

"For all I know, he could be, if he was the blackmailer, or if he knew about the blackmailing scheme."

We both ate for a moment. The monster dog was delicious, and so was the coleslaw that came with it. Then Jenny returned with a tall man in khakis and a white shirt. He approached the table and smiled politely.

"Jenny said you needed to talk to me about a former employee?" His voice was deep and a tad put-out. "I'm Brent Gilfoyle."

I set down my fork and thanked him for coming over. "I'm looking for a former employee of yours: Taylor Walsh."

"What's this about?" Brent asked.

Willie quietly ate her pizza, her head down. Brent waved at Jenny, and she walked away. I decided to be blunt.

"Taylor was involved in some kind of blackmailing scheme that took place a little over a year ago. I'm tracking him down on behalf of my client."

Brent's face went dark. "That happened in my restaurant?"

I nodded. "I don't know if Taylor was involved in taking money or if he was just a go-between. That's why I'd like to talk to him."

"This is bad." Brent lowered his voice. "I run a nice little restaurant; we have for decades. I don't want any trouble around here."

"I understand that," I said. "And I'm not accusing you of anything. I'd like to track down Taylor to find out what really happened, and what his involvement was."

"He doesn't work here anymore. Jenny told you that."

"Do you know where he lives?"

Brent hesitated, but I could tell he was relenting. It was the reason why I'd told him about the blackmailing in the hope that, if he wasn't involved, and I had no reason to think he was, he'd want to keep things clean, and so he'd cooperate.

"I'm sure I have his old records," Brent said. "Let me look up his address for you."

"Thank you," I said.

Brent turned away, then stalked across the room and disappeared down the hallway.

"You get Taylor's address and that will get you somewhere," Willie said. "It could end up being a short case for you, though. If you find out from Taylor who the blackmailer was, there you go."

I tipped my head skeptically. "You really think things will be that easy?"

Her brow wrinkled. "Knowing you, no."

"Oh, that's cold."

She reached a hand across the table. "Darling, I love you. But none of your cases ever end up being easy."

"And maybe you just jinxed me," I smirked.

We finished our meal, but Brent didn't return. Jenny brought the check. I was beginning to think Brent had blown me off, and then he emerged from the hallway and walked over. He handed me a piece of paper.

"This is the address for Taylor I have on file. I have no idea if he still lives there are not. I haven't had any contact with him since he quit."

"How about a phone number?"

He shook his head. "I don't have that anymore."

"Jenny indicated that he'd worked here for quite some time," I said. "Do you know why he quit?"

He shook his head. "He was a good employee, though. I was sorry to see him leave. He scowled. "I hope his leaving didn't have something to do with the blackmailing, that he was making money on that and he didn't need this job." He held up his hands. "I had no idea something like that was happening, and I would hate to think that Taylor knowingly participated in it. He was a nice guy, always good with the customers. Like I said, I was sorry to see him leave."

I looked at the address. "I appreciate your help."

Brent nodded, and I got the impression he hoped he wouldn't see me again. I paid the check, then looked at Willie and held up the piece of paper. "Let's hope this means a quick ending. I can go talk to Taylor tonight, if he's around, and find out what's going on."

"Then we should take a few days off," she said.

"Sure."

How wrong we both were.

CHAPTER FIVE

Willie and I walked out of the restaurant and I looked around. She must've seen the look on my face, and she put her hands on her hips.

"What're you thinking?"

I was remembering what Dennis had told me. "Dennis made three blackmail deliveries before he lost his house and job. I asked him if he confronted Taylor at any point, and he said the last time he asked Taylor what he was doing with the envelope. Taylor ignored him and took the envelope. That time, when Taylor went into the kitchen, Dennis ran outside, but the hostess stopped him because he hadn't paid for his meal." I walked to the side of the building and peered around the corner. Then I pointed. "There's an alley down there." I headed down the sidewalk and Willie called out after me.

"Wait!" She caught up to me. "Then what happened?"

I reached the alley entrance. "Dennis walked into the alley and looked around the corner like this," I demonstrated what he'd told me and peered into the gloom. "He saw Taylor smoking a cigarette by the back door. He couldn't tell if Taylor had the envelope or not."

I continued to look into the alley. Willie peeked around my

shoulder and waited a minute, then whispered, "What happened next?"

"He said that ..." I was whispering as well, then I stopped and spoke in a normal voice. "Taylor finished his cigarette and went back into the restaurant. Dennis has no idea what Taylor did with the envelope. Dennis raced back into the restaurant, but his table had been cleared. He confronted Taylor, but Taylor said he didn't know anything, just that he was supposed to take the envelope outside and put it in a stack of crates behind the dumpster."

Willie stepped past me and tiptoed into the alley. "That's it?"

"Dennis tried to get Taylor to tell him more, but Taylor got angry and walked away. Dennis waited, but he didn't have an opportunity to talk to Taylor again. Dennis watched the alley for a while, but didn't see anyone else."

Willie turned to me, her lips pressed into a pensive line. "You don't have much to go on."

I shook my head. "I don't. I came here because I wanted to see the blackmail drop, and then I'll start talking to Dennis's family, his coworkers, his ex-wife, and any friends I can track down. Someone had to have known he was stealing from his company, and hopefully I can find that person. Or people." I looked at the back door of the restaurant. "Or, if I can find Taylor Walsh, he might be able to shed more light on what happened."

Willie walked over and took my hand. "Good luck with that. Right now, I'm really tired. Do you think we could go home?"

I nodded and kissed her. "Yes. I'll work on this later." I held up the piece of paper that Brent Gilfoyle had given me. "Although I do want to drop by Taylor Walsh's apartment to see if I can talk to him. Do you mind?"

Her eyes creased with disappointment. "I was hoping for an evening with you."

"I need to see whether he might be home at night. More likely than daytime. I'll be home pretty soon."

"Sure," she said.

I walked her to her car. "Is everything okay?"

She nodded. "I'm tired is all."

I studied her, not sure what was going on. She usually didn't mind some time to herself when she got home from work. "Okay."

She didn't say more, so I watched her drive away, then got in the 4-Runner and put the address Gilfoyle had given me into the GPS.

On the way to Taylor Walsh's place, I thought about Dennis Mowery. He was certainly down on his luck, and in some ways, he reminded me of my noir hero, Humphrey Bogart in one of the best film noir movies ever, *In A Lonely Place*. He played Dixon Steele, a screenwriter with a temper who's accused of murder. His beautiful neighbor, played by Gloria Grahame, provides his alibi, and they, of course, fall in love. However, Steele's self-doubt and rage sabotage the relationship. The movie ending is classic film noir, dark and disturbing. I love Bogie's portrayal of Sam Spade and Philip Marlowe, some of noir's greatest detectives – tortured men trying to escape their demons. I had the feeling Dennis had demons of his own that he wasn't telling me about, and I wondered if he'd be able to move beyond his troubled past.

I soon reached Taylor Walsh's four-story apartment building off Colfax Avenue and Yosemite Street. At least, I hoped he still lived here. The place was drab yellow brick with a small front lawn starving for water. I found a bank of mailboxes near a stairwell, but none was labeled. I climbed stairs to 302 and knocked on the door and waited. When no one answered, I knocked again. Then I peered into a window, but the curtains were closed and I couldn't see inside. I tried the apartments on both sides, but no one was home. I went downstairs and looked around for a manager's office. I finally found it at the back, knocked, but got no answer there, either. I was striking out. Some kids rode by on bikes as I returned to my car. I was tempted to ask them if they knew Taylor Walsh, but then realized I didn't have a good description of him. Some detective I was. I slipped behind the wheel, then googled Dennis's wife, Kim. She lived in Golden, on the opposite side of the city. I wanted to talk to her, but then thought about Willie.

Her mood was off, so I thought better of working too late tonight, and I headed home. We live in the Uptown neighborhood, northeast of downtown. When I got there, our downstairs neighbors, Ace and Deuce Smith, were just leaving.

"Hey Reed," Ace said. His light gray eyes danced.

"How're you doing?" Deuce asked. The brothers aren't twins, but they could be, with the same dirty blond hair, the same gray eyes. I've known them for years and think of them as family, and years ago, I affectionately dubbed them the Goofball Brothers. They both have their talents, and they're certainly not dumb, but it sometimes seems that they're a few books short of a library.

"We're going to shoot some pool at B-52s," Ace said. "Want to come along?"

I shook my head. "I'd love to, but I need to do some work." As much as I would've loved to go to B-52s, a pool hall within walking distance of our building, Willie was tired, and I needed to get home to her.

Both brothers nodded in unison. "Okay," Deuce said. "If you need our help, you let us know."

"I will," I said.

I'd often had the Goofballs help me on cases, although it was a challenge at times because they didn't want to do anything they considered "boring." I could relate, I thought as I watched them disappear around the side of the building. I smiled. They were changing, growing up even? They had recently told me they were taking a couple of freshman classes at Metropolitan State College. I hadn't realized they were interested in getting college degrees. Ace has worked his way up to manager at a Best Buy, and he'd told me he didn't want to stay there forever. He wasn't sure what he *did* want to do, but he figured a degree might help. And Deuce had expressed an interest in starting his own construction company. I knew their older brother, Bob, was watching over them, advising them and helping to guide them on what was best. I was also impressed that the Goofballs were willing to go after what they wanted. Geez, I might have to quit thinking of them as "the Goofballs." I heard their voices fade, and I went upstairs and was greeted by our young cat, Humphrey, named after Bogart. He was a stray kitten that I'd picked up during an investigation a year or so ago. Willie and I love him dearly, and I'm only slightly jealous when she pays more attention to Humphrey than to me.

"Hey, little boy," Willie said as she came out from the kitchen. She scooped up Humphrey and nuzzled his face. He immediately began purring, and he shot me a look that seemed to emphasize what I'd just been thinking. He was getting all the attention and he loved it.

"I'm going to change clothes and watch a little TV," Willie said.

"How about a film noir?" I suggested. "This case, and Dennis Mowery, got me thinking about that Bogart classic called *In a Lonely Place* ..."

Willie frowned at me. "Sweetie, I think I'll pass on film noir tonight. I'd just like to watch something a little lighter, if you don't mind."

"Of course." I nodded. "It's no problem."

Willie did her best to humor me when it came to film noir and my love of Bogie. But not everyone held the same appreciation for those movies that I did. I watched her petting Humphrey, and I still couldn't gage her mood. I pointed down the hallway.

"I've got a little work to do anyway. I'll join you in a while, if that's okay?"

"Sure." She carried Humphrey to the couch and sat down.

I got a Fat Tire from the refrigerator, kicked off my shoes, and went into my office. I sat down at my desk and took a sip of the beer. Then I looked around to gather my thoughts. Along with my shelves of books and DVDs, I have three treasured original movie posters on the walls: *The Maltese Falcon* and *The Big Sleep*, both starring Bogart, and *The Postman Always Rings Twice*, with Lana Turner and John Garfield. Willie had given me the last one as a wedding present. As I often did, I hoped staring at the posters would give me some inspiration. When nothing occurred to me, I got on the internet and spent some time looking up Taylor Walsh on Facebook and other social media sites. Unfortunately, his was a common name for both males and females, and there were several people with pages. I perused a few of them, but wasn't sure I had the right Taylor. I finally gave up. I took a sip of beer, then picked up my cell phone and called Cal. To say he's a computer whiz is an understatement. He works in cybersecurity and often knows more about the cyber-world than most of us ever will. With his expertise, he could find the correct Taylor Walsh, and he'd get the information much faster than I could. However, he didn't answer. I was not getting anywhere tonight. I left him a message to call me, then looked up Mowery Transportation. It had been family owned for forty years, and it serviced several western states. I clicked on the "About" page, and read a little bit more about Dennis's father, Grant. He was sixty-one years old and had begun as a truck driver before starting Mowery Transportation. I also read about Isaac, Dennis's younger brother. Isaac had gone to the University of Colorado and had previously worked at a trucking company in Ohio. The website had pictures of both, and I could see a resemblance to Dennis, although Isaac's hair was shorter and his face rounder. I wanted to talk to both of them about Dennis to see if they knew anything about his stealing from the company, or the blackmail. I did a little more research on both, found nothing interesting, and finally stopped. I grabbed my beer and went into the living room. Willie was lying down on the couch with Humphrey nuzzled up near her.

"Did you figure it all out?" She yawned as she paused the TV.

"Hardly," I said as I snuggled up next to her. "I've got a lot of running around to do tomorrow, a lot of people to talk to. Someone knew what Dennis was up to, and I'm going to have to do some digging to find out who."

"I've got to work, too," she said. Humphrey stretched and got up. "Ouch, Humphrey." She impatiently pushed him aside. "Will you let me know if you'll be available for dinner?"

I stared at her for a second. She was usually way more affectionate with Humphrey, no matter what he did. "You got it." I hesitated. "Is everything okay?"

A cloud passed over her face, and then she forced a smile. "I just miss you."

"Okay." I finally looked to the TV. "What are we watching?"

"It's a sitcom about a couple who live in New York." She shifted to get more comfortable. "See that guy with the black hair? He works in finance ..."

She sounded a lot like me when I try to give her the synopsis of a film noir movie. I put my arm around her and we watched TV until we both nodded off.

CHAPTER SIX

The next morning, Willie was out the door early. Then Humphrey gave me some attention as I ate breakfast. He got up on the table and tried to drink out of my cereal bowl, and I pulled him onto my lap, where he kneaded and purred. I showered and dressed, and went down the hall to my office. Humphrey curled up on a cat bed on the desk while I researched Dennis Mowery. I didn't find any social media accounts – not that I expected to – and the only thing I did find was a LinkedIn page with Dennis's work history at Mowery Transportation. The page also showed that he'd gone to the University of Florida. He'd worked for an accounting firm in Miami before taking over the accounting side of things at his dad's company. I was about to get a cup of coffee when my phone rang.

"O Great Detective," Cal greeted me in his nasally voice. "I take it from your message you're on a new case."

"Yep." I told him about my visit with Dennis and his sister, Michelle. Humphrey didn't seem to like my talking on the phone, and he batted my hand while I talked.

"A blackmailer?" he said when I finished. "It doesn't sound like you have much to go on."

"I don't. Can you look up Taylor Walsh? I have his address, but not a phone number. I found a number of Taylor Walshes in the metro area, but I'm having trouble narrowing them down to the correct one."

I heard the clack of him typing as I talked. His fingers on a keyboard were like a pianist's on a piano. I put Humphrey back in his bed, and he laid down with his back to me. Rejected.

"Okay," Cal said slowly after a minute. "Based on the address, I've found the right Walsh. He's thirty years old, and it looks like he's an avid skier."

"How'd you find that out?"

"Elementary, my dear Watson."

"Ha." Even though I'm the detective and he's the sidekick, he really is the Sherlock Holmes to my Dr. Watson. "There are a lot of Taylor Walshes, or variations of that name, on Facebook, but I've got some software that compared the accounts to his address information."

"I don't even want to know about that."

He snickered. "I'll email you a link to his Facebook page. I'm not finding anything remarkable one way or the other. He doesn't have a criminal record, no marriage or divorce records, but I do have a phone number."

He gave that to me, and I jotted it down. "Can you find a number for Kim Mowery?" I spelled the last name. "I don't think she remarried after she divorced Dennis."

"Hang on." More typing, then he said, "Here you go."

I wrote that down as well. "Okay, Holmes, do you have time to check on Dennis?" I asked. "And his relatives. Michelle Farley, and their father, Grant, and the brother, Isaac? All the usual stuff, their backgrounds, any criminal records, that kind of thing?"

"Sure. I'm working with a new client, but it's all the usual stuff, and I'm not too busy at the moment. I can whip this out pretty quickly."

"If I need surveillance, I'll let you know. The Goofballs hate helping me with that."

"Nope. No way."

I laughed. "How's everything going?"

"Holly and I are going to a Rockies game later this week."

My ultra-reclusive friend had come out of his shell since he'd met Holly

Durocher, his girlfriend. We'd met Holly when she needed help after her grandmother had been murdered, and Cal had been smitten. Holly owns Sunshine Cupcakes in Golden, a suburb nestled in the foothills west of downtown, and Cal often leaves his house in the mountains to visit her. He even takes more care with his appearance, another fun change.

"Thanks for everything," I said.

"Always happy to do it, as long as you don't put me in dangerous situations."

"That's only happened a time or two," I protested. Okay, maybe more times than I was willing to admit.

"I'll call you later." He ended the call.

Now that I had a number for Taylor Walsh, I called it. Unfortunately, I got a standard voice-mail greeting, so I didn't even get to hear what Taylor's voice sounded like. I decided not to tip my hand and leave a message. I checked my email and clicked on the link that Cal had sent, which opened Taylor's Facebook page. He was tall and slim, his blond hair about shoulder-length. He had striking blue eyes and a wide smile. As Cal had said, Taylor did appear to be an avid skier, as many of his posts showed him on the slopes. His relationship status was single, and he didn't list jobs or other personal information, just pictures of him skiing, or with friends.

I tried Kim Mowery next, but didn't get an answer from her, either, so I looked up Rockridge Architecture, where she worked. I called that number, and a clipped male voice answered.

"Rockridge Architecture."

"I'd like to speak to Kim Mowery, please."

"She's at a job site this morning."

"Where is that?"

"Let me transfer you." He was as deft as I was at dodging questions. I was prepared to leave a voice mail when a woman answered.

"This is Kim."

I introduced myself and said, "I'm a private investigator."

"Oh, I thought you were the inspector calling to say he's late. Am I in some kind of trouble?" The tone was skeptical.

"I'm helping out Dennis, your ex-husband. His sister, Michelle ..."

That's as far as I got before she interrupted. "Dennis? He fell off the face of the earth a little over a year ago. He isn't dead?"

"No, he's alive and sober."

She swore softly. "I didn't think that would ever happen." The tone was a combination of things, and none of it seemed good. "Oh, the inspector's here. Can I call you back?"

"Could we meet in person?"

A sigh. "Sure. I'm at a job site." She gave me the address. "If you can get here in the next half-hour, I can talk." It was obvious she was used to giving the orders.

"I'll see you soon."

She ended the call before I could say goodbye. I gave Humphrey a quick petting, then grabbed my keys and left.

I'd wanted to stop by Taylor Walsh's apartment again, but I needed to catch Kim while she was willing to talk, so I beelined up Interstate 25. The job site Kim referred to was an office building in Broomfield, north of downtown. I parked across the street from the site, then walked to a chain-link fence and onto the property. I heard construction sounds to the left, metal clanking on metal, and walked that way. Then a voice called out.

"Hey!"

I turned around to see a woman in tight jeans and a blue blouse walking toward me. She had high cheekbones, a thin nose, and dark eyes. A hardhat covered long hair the color of dry grass. She held a metal clipboard.

"Kim?" I asked.

She held out a hand. "You must be Reed Ferguson. Follow me." I walked with her inside the building and down a hallway to stairs. "I couldn't believe you mentioned Dennis," she called over her shoulder. "And he's sober?"

"By your tone, you don't seem pleased about that," I said as we climbed to the second floor.

We entered an unfinished room. The whine of a saw drifted

through open window frames. Dust was all over the place. Kim looked around, then sniffed.

"After all that man put me through, it wouldn't have bothered me if he was dead. I'm sure that surprises you for me to say so, but he turned into a horrible husband, and he ruined what could've been a great marriage. He had everything going for him, and he threw it all away." She consulted her clipboard and frowned. "This isn't correct," she muttered.

"Wait a minute. I thought you had a good marriage."

"Who told you that?" She raised an eyebrow in a disarming way. "Dennis?" I nodded, and she made a derisive noise. "Of course he did. It started out all right, but I think he cheated on me. And then there was the drinking and drugging."

"He was unfaithful?"

She gave that some thought. "I don't know that for sure, but his behavior was odd. He sometimes wouldn't come home, then he'd say he had to work late and that he slept at the office. I didn't buy it."

"It could've been because of the drinking and drugging."

"I suppose, but it felt different from that. And he could get violent. He never actually hit me, but he has a wicked angry streak."

Not what I'd heard from Dennis. I'd have to follow up with him on that part. She walked across the room, to an area that didn't have flooring. I stayed where I was.

"Do you know what pushed him over the edge?"

Her lips were a hard line. "I know he blamed it on getting pain pills after his knee surgery, but I think it was more than that. Plenty of people take pain pills and don't have any problems, so why would that throw him into a tailspin?"

I shrugged. "It's hard to explain addictions."

"And it's hard to explain stupidity," she snapped. She finally looked at me. "I begged him to get some help, to do something, but he wouldn't. He kept drinking more and more, and got more and more out of control. I finally couldn't take it anymore, and I threw him out."

"He never tried AA or anything like that while he was with you?"

She shook her head. "I tried Al-Anon, the group for friends and relatives of an addict, but it didn't really help. I reached a point where

I wasn't willing to just accept his behavior, and we were fighting constantly. It was not a happy time, and I refused to live that way. That's when I told him he had to get clean and sober, or I would throw him out and change the locks. He chose booze and pills over me, and he moved into a motel." She pointed a finger at me. "Is he trying to blame me?" She walked across the room and looked out a window. Her spine was stiff, her anger evident.

"No," I said. "From what I can tell, he's taking ownership for his actions." Or almost, if what she'd said about his temper and affairs was true. "One of the things he shared with me is that he was being blackmailed."

She whirled around. "Blackmailed? For what?" Her voice echoed across the room.

"He'd been skimming off the books. He needed money for his addictions, and then money to pay the blackmailer – or blackmailers."

"Oh really?"

The grumbling of a truck rattled the building as I studied her. "You didn't know that?"

"He needed money?" she repeated.

I eyed her. "How did you think he paid for his addictions?"

She shrugged. "With our money, at first. We both had access to our checking and savings accounts, and then we had a big blowout because he'd taken a lot of money out of the savings account. At that point I set up my own separate accounts, and I told him I was transferring the money into that. We fought over it, but I did it anyway. Then he didn't have access to anything."

"And he had to get money not just from his paychecks, but from somewhere else," I speculated.

"That was his problem." Her footsteps were loud, angry, as she walked back toward me. "I didn't know what he was doing. I was so frustrated dealing with him being drunk and high all the time, and that's not an easy thing. Have you ever lived with an alcoholic?"

"No." I shrugged.

"It's hard, and if you think I'm going to feel sorry for him, you're wrong. I have a good thing going here," she waved a hand around, "and

I did when we were married. I wasn't going to let him or anybody else ruin that."

"You never had any indication that Dennis was in trouble, that somebody was blackmailing him?"

She softened slightly as she thought about that. "One time, we were fighting and Dennis said something was going on, that he was in trouble, but he never said what. I thought he meant something with his work, but when I asked him about it, he didn't say. He was drunk, so it was hard to know what was really going on."

"Did he elaborate about the trouble he was in?"

She shook her head. "No. He mentioned it just the once, and he never said what that was about."

I wasn't sure I believed her. "You got along with Dennis's family?"

"Yes. Michelle's nice, and so are her husband and kids. She has two boys, Andy and Jordan. Jordan is in high school, and Andy's in college." She smiled. "Andy's quiet, smart. Jordan is a real pistol. But they're good kids. Dennis is different from his brother, Isaac. I always felt there was something between them, but Dennis didn't talk about it. Have you met Grant and Sheila, Dennis's parents?"

I shook my head. "Just Michelle."

"His parents weren't happy with Dennis, either."

"Who might've been blackmailing him?"

She shrugged. "Someone at his work, I would think."

"You're sure he never talked to you about stealing from the company? Maybe he slipped up when he was drunk, and then you told someone?"

"Of course not."

"He could've told someone else about his skimming off the books."

"True, but I don't know who that might've been."

I wasn't sure if I was reacting to her anger, but something about our interaction wasn't sitting well. "Any friends of his I should talk to?"

"His closest friend was John Talbot, but as far as I know, they lost contact when Dennis's drinking got out of control."

"Do you have a number for John?"

"No, sorry. Ask Dennis."

"I will. Could John have blackmailed Dennis?"

"I have no idea if he knew what Dennis was up to. I guess he could've. But John's a great guy. I don't see him doing something like that to his friend." She glanced at her phone. "Why are you looking into all this?"

"Michelle initially asked me to, but I wasn't going to until Dennis was willing to talk to me. That's when I found out about the blackmail. Michelle's worried that if Dennis doesn't make peace with his past, that might affect his sobriety."

"Maybe."

"What does that mean?"

She chose her words carefully. "Michelle wasn't happy with Dennis, and she encouraged her dad to fire Dennis. If she's saying she's sympathetic to Dennis now, that's a change."

"Interesting." I filed away that information.

"What's Dennis going to do when he finds the blackmailer?"

I was slow to respond. "That's a good question, and not one I can answer. I would hope he'd have peace knowing that that person has been caught."

She headed for the stairs. "If you want to poke around and help Dennis, that's your business. But as far as I'm concerned, he can drop dead. I don't want to have anything more to do with him."

I didn't say anything to that.

CHAPTER SEVEN

I sat in my car for a moment and mulled over what Kim Mowery had told me. She'd painted a very different picture of her marriage than either Dennis or Michelle had. I wondered what others thought of Dennis, so I decided to see if I could talk to people who knew Dennis now. It was hot and dry, so I cranked the air conditioner and got back on the interstate. I drove into downtown and parked on Larimer Street, then walked to Step Recovery. I entered a small room with inspirational posters on the walls and benches near the door. A strong cleanser smell hung heavy in the air. A man at a counter opposite the door looked up with a smile.

"May I help you?" He was older, with a goatee and dark eyes.

"I hope so," I said. I watched as a couple of men walked by. Both were clean-shaven, with neatly cut hair, but both also seemed older than one might've thought. They nodded politely at me as they went out the door. I turned back to the man at the counter. "I wanted to talk to you about Dennis Mowery."

His face revealed nothing. "If you're asking about a resident, I can't tell you anything. This is a recovery program and the privacy of our residents is important."

"I understand that, but Dennis has hired me to help him." I

showed him my private investigator's license. "Dennis didn't say anything about me?"

He again didn't commit to an answer. "I'm sorry, but I can't help you."

"Okay."

I looked around. Two men sat at the benches, one flipping through a magazine, the other staring into space. A poster on the wall near them read "Sober Life 4 Life." I turned back to the man at the counter.

"How do things operate here?"

"We take in men who don't have anywhere else to go, and we give them a chance." Now he was in his element, his dark eyes joyful. "We don't believe in government assistance, so we rely on private donations and on the men working. No one gets a free ride here." He smiled. "It seems to work. A lot of men make it in recovery, in large part because they're working on it. Not everyone agrees with our philosophy, but if it works for some, that's okay in my book."

"I see," I murmured. "So if Dennis was staying here, he would be working today?"

A slight smile. "As I've told you, sir, I can't say anything."

I smiled back. "Okay, thanks for your time."

I headed back outside. The sun gleamed as I stood on the sidewalk and wiped sweat from my brow. Then I started down the block toward my car.

"Hey," a voice said.

I turned around and saw the man who had been staring into space walking toward me. I stopped as he approached. He peeked over his shoulder, then limped up to me.

"You were asking about Dennis?" His voice was gravelly.

I nodded. "Yes. You know him?"

I caught a whiff of strong soap. He was clean, his clothes a little shabby, his face weathered and wrinkled. Another man who'd likely lived a hard life. He squinted at me.

"Is Dennis in some kind of trouble?" he asked.

I shook my head. "You overheard me?"

"Of course. You weren't talking softly."

"Good point." I waited, and he didn't say anything. I tipped my head to encourage him. "Did you need something?"

He glanced toward Step Recovery again, then tugged at my elbow. "Come on." He favored his right leg as we walked around the corner, and he stopped. "I don't want Jim at the desk to know I'm talking to you." He gave an exaggerated shrug. "It's not like I can't, but it would just be better."

"Why?"

"They're big on the anonymous part." His face scrunched up. "You're asking about Dennis, I thought I should tell you, you best be careful."

"Oh?"

A car slowed as it went by, and he stiffened. The driver seemed to be looking for a place to park, and it drove to the next corner and turned.

"What's your name?" I asked him.

"Frankie." He reached into his pocket for a cigarette. As he lit it, he said, "Addictions come in pairs with a spare."

I chuckled. "That's a new one on me."

"I've been sober for six months this time." He puffed on the cigarette and kept talking. "Dennis has been at Step for a few months now. In the first phase, you live with everybody else." He scratched chin stubble. "It's all right, I guess. A little like living in an army barracks, but it's better than being on the street. The guys snore more than I remember from the army. Anyway, he bunked next to me for a while. The rules are you have to work, and you have to go to AA meetings, and they like you to attend chapel services. They have one every night at eight, an early morning service, and some on the weekends." He shrugged. "You don't have to believe in God, but they emphasize a spiritual side. Anything that'll help get you sober. You hear a lot of stories from the guys, a lot of hard living on the streets and that kind of thing. But when it comes to Dennis ..."

I stared at him. "What? Don't worry, it'll stay here."

He rubbed his chin again. "Usually you see guys making some changes. They go from blaming everybody else to taking some responsibility for how their lives turned out. Hell, we all have things that knocked us down, got us where we were drinking or using too much. But at some point, you realize that you made some choices, too. But with Dennis, it's different. I'm still waiting for him to say he messed up. If you listen to him, it's always somebody else's fault. When he first arrived, there was a fight about which bed he'd get. It almost got violent." He gestured toward the side of the building. "Even around here, if something happens, he's quick to blame the other guy."

It sounded like a family spat, two brothers irritated at each other. But after talking to Kim, one thing stuck out. "Is Dennis violent?"

"He can fly off the handle." Frankie scowled. "I know what you're thinking, I got a beef with Dennis. But it's not just me. Most of the guys don't like him. He acts like he's better than the rest of us, and it feels like he's always looking for an angle, a way to scam the other guy." He took a drag on the cigarette. "I don't know why you're looking into him, but you need to be careful. You can't trust him."

"Why are you telling me this?"

His eyes narrowed. "You don't believe me." I didn't answer, and he went on, his manner conspiratorial. "I overheard him the other night on the phone. He was talking about keeping quiet."

"About what?"

He leaned back with a shrug. "I don't know. He saw me, and he cursed me out, said I should mind my own business. So I did."

"Where is Dennis now?" I asked.

"He's working. That's another thing. He's in construction now, and he doesn't like it. He thinks just because he's sober that now he should go back to whatever he was doing before. He doesn't get why people don't want to hire him on the spot, even though they can tell there's something odd about him. He's gotta do his time getting clean, just like the rest of us."

I gave him a quick once-over. "Just out of curiosity, why aren't you working?"

He gestured toward his leg. "I hurt my leg last week. I can't work construction now." Another drag on the cigarette. "I got more hard years than Dennis, and I can't keep up like I used to. I'm going to have to figure out something, though. They don't like it if you're not working. Not that they'll throw me out right away, but I gotta figure out a way to pay my rent." He pointed with the cigarette. "I'm not complaining, it's just the way it is." He looked toward the street. "Anyway, I gotta get going. You be careful with whatever you're doing, okay?"

I nodded and thanked him. "I'll be careful. You, too."

He gave me a sad look, turned and limped around the corner.

CHAPTER EIGHT

I had only talked to two people about Dennis, so I still had more questions than answers. Frankie had confirmed Dennis wasn't at Step Recovery at the moment, so I would have to talk to Dennis later. I needed to follow up with him because he'd given me a different picture of his behavior from what others saw. If he was hiding something from me, I was going to find out what. I was walking back to my car when a familiar voice said, "Oh, it's not always easy to know what to do." It was my ringtone: Humphrey Bogart as Sam Spade in a line from *The Maltese Falcon*. I didn't recognize the number, but picked up anyway.

"Is this Reed Ferguson?" A male voice, moderate tone, clipped.

"It is. Who is this?"

"This is Isaac Mowery, Dennis's brother. My sister hired you to help him. I don't know what you all expect to find out, but Kim said that you might want to talk to me."

I'd reached my car, and I unlocked it and got in. "Yes, I'd like to speak with you."

"How about now? Let's get this over with." The manner was all about command, with an almost defiant tone that dared me to put him off. I was certainly tempted to. I didn't respond well to being pushed around. However, I did want to talk to him, and so, as he said, I might as well get it over with.

"I'm free now," I said.

"Meet me at the company. You know we have a trucking business, right?"

"Yes, I do."

"Good." He gave me the address. "I'll be waiting for you."

"I'll be there soon."

I bit off a snide remark as I ended the call, then put the address into the GPS.

Mowery Transportation was located off Interstate 70, east of I-25. As I drove out of downtown, I got caught in traffic, and it took me about ten minutes longer than I initially expected. As I rounded a bend in the road, I saw several 18-wheelers lined up in a several-acre lot surrounded by a chain link fence. Beyond them were two tall warehouses with loading docks. At the end of the street, I turned into a paved lot and parked in front of an office. I was about to go inside when I heard someone holler my name. I turned and looked past a shiny black truck to see a man about my height – 6-foot – walk over. He wore jeans and had a thick chest that stretched the buttons on his short-sleeved blue shirt. His dark curly hair was trimmed short, and his smile was cold.

"I'm Isaac Mowery." He held out a hand and when I shook it, the grip was firm. He held the handshake a tad long, as if to let me know how strong he was. He waved a hand at me. "Come with me and we can talk."

"Sure."

I followed him past some of the 18-wheelers to the end of the lot. He pointed at a white semi truck without the trailer. "You ever been in one of these?"

I shook my head, wondering what he was up to. I had a bad vibe from him. I glanced around. We were alone.

"Come on," he said. "I have to take this one for a spin. We just completed some repairs on it, and I need to know if it's running smoothly."

His stomped up to the semi in his heavy boots. He grinned at me as he reached up and opened the driver's side door, then hopped up into the seat. I went around the front, glad that he hadn't started the rig yet. With the attitude he was conveying, I thought he might've run me over. I reached up for the door handle and somewhat gracelessly hefted myself in. Isaac was putting on his seatbelt, and he jammed a key in the ignition.

"Fasten your seatbelt."

I didn't like the way he said it, as if he were taking me for some kind of ride. Physically *and* mentally? I thought to myself. I put on my seatbelt. He donned dark sunglasses, then fired up the rig and eased away from the fence. I sat forward so I could see over the hood. The big rig rumbled across the lot and to the gate, the engine loud. Isaac turned right, shifted, and hit the gas.

"It's riding pretty smooth," he said.

To me, it was a bumpy ride. Isaac drove along the street, then slowed for a stoplight. I'd never sat up so high before, and it was different to look down on the other cars. He pulled up behind a BMW, and the closer he got, the less I could see of the car. It seemed that Isaac was showing off for me. The air brakes released with a loud hiss.

"So you're trying to help Dennis, huh?" he said. He glanced over at me, but I couldn't see his eyes behind the shades.

"Yes," I said.

"I'm not sure he deserves the help."

"Why is that?"

The light changed, and he pulled the rig forward. I could barely see the car in front of us.

"Dennis has always been a pain in the ass, even when we were kids," Isaac said. "He was cerebral – that's what our dad called it – wasn't into sports or things like that. But he always had a way of trying to show me up, trying to make it seem like he was smarter than me. Look where it got him. He ended up on the streets."

I rested an arm on the door as he took a corner a little too fast. "Did Dennis tell you what led to him drinking so much?"

He shifted gears and the rig picked up speed as he took an on-ramp onto the highway. "Dennis and I don't talk that much, but Michelle said he was into pills and booze." He glanced at me. "Then she told me a doozy this morning, that Dennis had been skimming off the books and that someone had been blackmailing him. And that led to some of the trouble right before Dad fired him."

"You don't sound too convinced of that."

He shook his head as we bounced along. "Dennis was stupid. He never should've paid the blackmailer. He should've come to us and told us that he was stealing from the company. I'm sure Dad would've fired him then, and Dennis would've deserved it. But wouldn't that have been better than the mess he got himself into?"

"How did you feel when you heard he'd been stealing from the company?" I subtly put my other hand on the seat as he picked up speed.

He swore. "What a scumbag. Stealing from the company, from your own dad? How do you think I feel? We all work hard to keep this business going, and Dennis shouldn't have done that. Just firing him was too good. He really ought to go to jail, don't you think?"

I shrugged. "That's not for me to say."

He quickly switched to the left lane, and I glanced in the side mirror. From my vantage point, it looked as if he'd cut off the car behind him. I guess he knew what he was doing, though. At least I hoped.

"He should go to jail," Isaac went on, "but I know Michelle and my dad won't do anything about it. They always treat him better than me."

"That frustrates you?"

He laughed. "I've gotten used to it. Dad always thought Dennis was smarter than I was, but he didn't respect the fact that I was good with my hands, good mechanically. But I've shown them. I know about the trucks. I can tear apart an engine and put it back together. And I have a good rapport with the drivers. That goes a long way, you know."

I nodded. "You didn't know Dennis was stealing from the company at the time? No hint of anything?"

He shook his head. "We trusted Dennis. All the bills were being paid, so how would I have known what was going on?"

"Michelle didn't know?"

"Nope. None of us."

"I know you just found out about the blackmailing, but any idea of somebody in the company who might have done that to Dennis?"

He switched lanes again and headed for an exit. "It could be anybody that found out what he was doing. The office manager, Clyde Hessler, could've known. Now did he? I don't know. Or somebody could've overheard Dennis talking about what he was doing and went after him."

"I've wondered that. Dennis said he was pretty hazy in the last several months before he lost his job. Maybe he told someone?"

He glanced over. "He didn't tell me."

"Was there anybody that Dennis didn't get along with?"

He turned onto Quebec Street, quickly enough that I again felt as if he were trying to scare me.

"Dennis was quiet and mostly stayed to himself, but he did clash with one of my technicians, Warren Singletary."

"Oh? What happened?"

"I came out to one of the warehouses to check on a few things. Dennis and Warren were arguing, but when they saw me, they both shut up. I asked them what was going on, and they said it was nothing." He frowned. "It didn't sound like nothing. They were angry. Warren even cursed me out, which wasn't smart to do to the boss."

I caught the threat in his tone. "What did Dennis do?"

He glanced away. "He got angry and left."

"That's it?"

"Yes, that's it. I didn't push it. I know him. Unless he was three sheets to the wind – which he wasn't – he wasn't going to tell me what was going on."

My gut said Isaac wasn't telling me everything. I pushed him a little, but he didn't elaborate, so I tried another approach. "Did you ask Warren about the argument?"

He shook his head. "I did. He apologized for speaking to me like he did, but he dismissed the argument as nothing. Something happened, though."

"Is Warren still with the company?"

"No, he left around the same time as Dennis. I don't know where he went."

"Interesting."

"If you say so." He stopped at a light and turned the sunglasses on me.

"What was it like growing up?" I asked. "Did Dennis pick on you?"

A sly grin crossed his face. "He tried. Once I got as big as him, he stopped."

I wondered what it must've been like living with Isaac, who had such a huge chip on his shoulder. "And how did Michelle fit into the sibling dynamics?"

"The dynamics," he repeated with a snide laugh. "Michelle is a peacemaker, and she tried to get the two of us to get along. But she favored Dennis back then, just like she does now."

I ventured a guess. "You think there's more to her hiring me than just wanting Dennis to stay sober?"

He slowed the rig and turned another corner. Up ahead I could see the trucking company lot.

"Michelle feels sorry for Dennis, and she wants to make up for the things that happened before."

"What things?"

His tongue ran over his lower lip. "She was frustrated with Dennis, tired of his behavior." He was holding something back, but before I could ask, he said, "Dennis wants everything to be back the way it was. But I don't know if I want him to come work for the company again. How could we trust him?"

"What did your parents think about Dennis with all his drinking and troubles?"

"They felt bad. My mom wondered what they'd done that might've made him drink, if they raised him wrong. I kept telling her that she shouldn't think like that. My dad was disappointed, one of his kids not able to handle his drinking, screwing up at the company. He didn't want to let Dennis go, but he had to. It didn't look good, letting the son get away with mistakes, being drunk on the job."

"What about Kim?"

"Dennis's ex? She's nice enough, put up with a lot more than I ever would've."

"Are you married?"

"Yeah. I have one son, Michael. He's a senior in high school. I want him to start learning the ropes here. If Michelle will allow it."

"Why wouldn't she?"

"She has more control than she should. She directs Dad on what should happen." He slowed the rig and careened into the parking lot, drove down to the end, and backed into a space. He cut the engine and turned to me. "You can look into Dennis all you want, and look into this blackmail thing, too. It won't change the fact that Dennis made mistakes. If he wants to stay clean and sober, he's going to have to suck it up and do it. He can't go looking for excuses."

"What excuses did he have before?"

He snorted. "Nothing is ever his fault. It's always the other guy. But sometimes you have to take responsibility for yourself."

He sounded like Frankie from Step Recovery. Isaac reached for the handle to get out, so I did the same. I hopped down to the ground and walked around the front of the rig. He put his hands on his hips as he stared at me. All I saw was my reflection in his sunglasses.

"I don't know who blackmailed Dennis, and a part of me doesn't believe that's even true," he said. "I do hope you figure everything out, what's going on with him, and I hope he does stay sober. But don't look to me for any more help. I'm busy, and I have a lot to do."

With that, he spun on his heel and walked toward a warehouse. He didn't bother looking back, but opened the door and disappeared inside.

"Very interesting," I murmured to nobody as I walked toward the office.

CHAPTER NINE

I was crossing the parking lot when Michelle Farley came out the office front door, her face panicky.

"Oh my gosh. What happened with Isaac?" She stared down the parking lot. "He didn't give you a hard time, did he?"

I raised an eyebrow. "You ask as if you think that might be the case."

She forced a smile. "I guess I didn't tell you that sometimes Isaac can be a little ... intense. And he wasn't very happy to find out that I'd hired a detective."

"Yes, I got that."

Two burly men in jeans and polo shirts with the company logo walked by. They exchanged quick pleasantries with Michelle, and she kept the smile plastered on her face. They headed for a warehouse, and when they were out of earshot, she wagged a finger at me to follow her into the office. "Let's go inside where we can talk in private."

I followed her into the building. The main room held three desks, a few chairs against a wall, and a large plant in the corner. A woman I gauged to be in her mid-twenties sat behind the closest desk, a headset on, talking on the phone. The other two desks were empty. The woman barely gave us notice. Michelle gestured for me to follow her down a short hallway and into an office. It was better decorated than the drab white of the main room, with soft cream-colored walls, and a picture of a sailboat hanging on one of them. A window looked out toward another warehouse. Michelle walked around an oak desk and sat down, then indicated for me to take a chair across from her. She sucked in a breath and blew it out in exasperation.

"What a morning this has been," she said. "I was met with problems at the office, and then we had a quick meeting to let everyone know about what Dennis had done, and about the blackmailing. We need to get to the bottom of things, and I don't want any secrets. I told everyone that if they have any information about a blackmailer, they can talk to me or to you."

I nodded thoughtfully. "I'll want to talk to your staff."

"I assumed you would, and you can do that today, if you want. I talked to Isaac earlier, and he wasn't happy."

I rested a hand on the armrest. The office was quiet and cool. I hadn't had time to gather my thoughts after talking to Isaac, so I did so now. "When did you catch up with Dennis?"

She took a sip of coffee, then set the cup down. "I'm sorry; would you like something to drink?" I shook my head and waited. She went on. "Dennis called last night and told me what happened. I was so relieved that he was willing to work with you. I was trying not to show it, but I was beside myself when he didn't show up for our meeting yesterday. I thought I'd scared him away, that he would worry about what I thought of him, and that he'd started drinking again." She picked up a pen and began fiddling with it. "It sounds like you guys had a good conversation, and you convinced him that he needed help."

I crossed one leg over the other. "I don't know what I convinced him of, but I got quite a story from him. What did he tell you?"

Her face fell. "He told me about the blackmailing, and about stealing from the company. From his family! Can you believe it? I have to say, I was shocked and disappointed. I would've never thought Dennis capable of stealing, but he said he needed the money to support his addictions." She clicked the pen, agitated, then set it down. "He's a great accountant, and he certainly fooled me. I had no idea what he was doing."

I stared at her. "Apparently, somebody did, and they used it to their advantage."

"I've been thinking about that all night." She drummed the desktop with her fingers for a moment. "I don't know who would've blackmailed him. But we have several people here in the office working in various capacities, and we have a lot of truck drivers. I suppose any one of them could have found out what Dennis had been doing."

"How would they have found out?"

"Dennis told me a bit about how he cooked the books. If he'd done something odd, created financial irregularities with our business partners, other employees have access to those records and they might've caught something fishy. Or if someone saw odd bank deposits or withdrawals. At times, Dennis needed help with the books. If he slipped extra expenses into a bid, then skimmed those off the books later, someone might've noticed." She wagged her head sadly. "Or Dennis might've slipped up and told someone what he was doing. I don't think he remembers half of what he did the last several months before he was fired."

My skeptical look remained. "You never picked up on anything?"

The fingers stopped drumming. "I've given it a lot of thought since he told me last night, and I can't come up with anything. His behavior got stranger as time went on, but I don't look at the books that much. I even asked Dad about it, and he didn't notice anything unusual. But then, Dad said he's not the numbers guy, and that's why he had Dennis doing it."

"Speaking of your dad, I do want to talk to him."

"Of course. He's meeting with another company at their office today. Why don't I schedule some time for you to talk to him tomorrow morning, say nine?"

"That'll be fine."

She made a note, then looked up. "I need to pay you."

"Yes." We discussed my fee, which is a flat daily rate plus expenses, and she said she'd get a check cut and mailed to me. Then I said, "Now that you know about Dennis stealing from the company, what do you intend to do about it?" I had one answer from Isaac, but I wanted to see if it matched hers.

She sat back and thought for a moment. "I'm sure Isaac gave you an earful." There was no fooling her. "He was pissed off when I told him what Dennis had done, and he was furious when I said it wouldn't do any good to press charges now." An annoyed sigh. "I'm not happy with what Dennis did, but he doesn't have any money now, so what would we go after? And to put him in jail wouldn't do any good, either. I'd rather see him get back on his feet, and maybe he could pay us back then. I told Isaac that, but it didn't seem to placate him." She crossed her arms. "Dennis and Isaac have never gotten along. I'm sure I don't know the extent of it. I thought Isaac would be happy that Dennis is clean and sober, but that doesn't seem to be the case."

"Was there something that happened in their past that led to this animosity between them?"

She hesitated. "It's just brotherly stuff, the competition. Nothing out of the ordinary."

I wasn't sure about that, and I figured it would be good to ask Dennis about his relationship with Isaac. She thought for a second and went on.

"Isaac has always thought that Dennis was treated better, but to be honest with you, Isaac was the spoiled one, the youngest. My parents doted on him as much as they ever doted on Dennis."

"Could Isaac have been behind the blackmail? You think he wanted to destroy his brother?"

"No." She was emphatic. "They may not get along, but Isaac would never do that. I even asked Isaac, and he denied it. He's the one person within the family who doesn't ever consult the books."

I didn't want to get into sibling rivalry at the moment, so I switched gears. "Isaac thinks you were the force behind getting Dennis fired."

She shook her head. "That's not true. I advised Dad, but it was his decision."

"Were you tired of Dennis's behavior?"

"Of course. I guess I could've come across as frustrated with him, but that doesn't mean I pushed for him to get fired." Guilt in her voice. "Isaac thinks I have too much power around here, but that's not the case."

Her tone said that was all on that subject, so I circled back to something. "Who all would've had access to the books, the record-keeping, back then?"

"All of us in the family, and our office manager, Clyde Hessler. He helped with the accounting then, and now he oversees it all. And after all this with Dennis, we'll be hiring an outside firm as well. You should talk to Clyde, although he's off today."

"A scheduled day off?"

She shook her head. "He's sick. You don't think he would've been involved?"

I shrugged. "I have to look at everything."

"Oh, sure, but I've known Clyde for several years. He'd never blackmail Dennis."

I let the comment slide. "Do you have Clyde's phone number?"

"Can't *it* wait? He took a day off."

"I really need to talk to everyone, the sooner the better."

"Fine." She looked on her phone, then wrote down a number and handed it to me.

I pocketed it, then said, "Who else should I talk to?"

"My uncle – Ben – is our safety manager, and he's part owner. There are a lot of regs he has to keep up with, and he works fairly closely with Isaac." Her eyes widened. "My gosh, you think it could be someone in the family?" Before I could answer, she gave a curt headshake. "I don't buy that for a second, but you ask away. We have no secrets here."

"Fine," I said. We were covering a lot quickly, and I returned to a previous topic. "You told your dad about what Dennis did?"

She nodded. "Dennis was too embarrassed to talk to my parents, so I did. Both Dad and Mom were disappointed, but they agree with me that it wouldn't do any good to go after Dennis now."

Her door opened and a young man with dark hair and eyes stopped short. His cheeks colored.

"Oh," he said with a curious gaze at me, "I didn't know you were with someone."

She waved a hand at him. "I'm busy, Andy. Can it wait?"

"Uh, yeah. Sorry. Since my car's in the shop, I was wondering if I can go to lunch with you later."

"Yes, or you can take your father's car. We'll talk later."

"Uh, right." The pink tint remained on his cheeks as he backed up and shut the door. She looked at me.

"My son. He works fulltime for us in the summer, then cuts back his hours when he's in school. CU."

"Ah," I said.

"It's a family business, in more ways than one. Most of us get along well, and we have great retention. People like working for us." She gave a quick wag of her head as if to clear her thoughts. "I think I've covered everything. Dennis told you about how he passed off the blackmail money?"

"Yes." I gave her an update on what I knew so far, which wasn't much. "Do you know Warren Singletary? He's one of your technicians."

She shook her head. "Did Isaac mention him?"

"Yes. He and Dennis had an argument when Dennis was still working here, but Isaac didn't know about what."

A small shrug. "When it comes to the drivers and technicians, I don't know them all by name."

"Singletary doesn't work here anymore."

"Oh."

"Dennis didn't mention a fight with him?"

"No." She sighed and changed the subject. "So, do you think you'll be able to find whoever blackmailed Dennis?"

I hedged my bets. "It's been a while ago, and although it's early, I'm having trouble tracking down the waiter who was the go-between. And there are a lot of suspects, so to speak. I wouldn't get your hopes up."

Her eyes filled with disappointment. "I understand, but it's worth a try."

I couldn't think of anything else to ask at the moment, so I said, "Could I talk to your staff now?"

"Absolutely. Let me introduce you to the receptionist, Christie Costa." She spelled the name for me. "After you talk to her, she can take you around to talk to everyone else."

She stood up and walked me back into the main room.

CHAPTER TEN

Christie Costa was still sitting at her desk in the main room. She had a round face that seemed rosier with her red blouse and alluring dark eyes. She offered me a cup of coffee. I declined.

"Reed wants to ask you a few questions about Dennis," Michelle said.

Christie put down her pen and looked at me. "Oh? If you think that's necessary." Her demeanor hinted at a chill even though she was being polite.

"Yes." Michelle pointed toward the hall. "Then introduce him around so he can talk to everyone else." With that, Michelle smiled at me and left.

Christie gave me a once-over, and I couldn't tell if she approved. "I really can't tell you anything more than you already know." I wasn't sure how she knew that, but I let her go on. "I didn't know anything about Dennis stealing from the company, and I didn't have a lot of contact with him, other than him coming and going. He was quiet. And I have no idea who might've known what he was doing."

Her condensed Q&A – without the Q – was nice, but I wasn't going to let her off that easily. I pressed her a bit on what the office was like when Dennis still worked at the company, and tried to see if there was something she might not have remembered. The most I got was that she knew Dennis better than she'd initially said, that they were friendly around the office, but she never interacted with him outside of work, at happy hours or company gatherings. Her answers were vague, and I had a feeling she didn't like him. She had observed him take a downturn in the months before he'd been let go, so she hadn't been surprised when he was no longer with the company. She knew Warren Singletary, said Isaac didn't like him, but had never seen Singletary talking to Dennis. After questioning her, I concluded that she either didn't know anything about Dennis's embezzlement, or she was lying really well. I had her take me around the office to talk to a couple of dispatchers – Enrique and Sue – who were both busy and impatiently answered my questions.

"You've put us in a difficult position," Enrique said as he adjusted a headset.

I leaned against a door jamb. "How so?"

He glanced at Christie. "Come on, man, you want us to talk about the boss's son."

"I can see that," I said. "However, I've been hired to see who was blackmailing Dennis, and any information you have about that would be appreciated."

I thought I sounded smooth, but all I got was an irritated look from him.

"I didn't know anything," Sue said. "I'd see Dennis around, and I noticed his behavior. I smelled alcohol on his breath sometimes. But I had no idea that he was stealing from the company, or that he was being blackmailed." She finished with a shrug.

Enrique nodded agreement. I plowed on, and switched up my questions to see if anything changed in their responses, but nothing did. I again was left with the impression they didn't like Dennis, and neither knew anything about Singletary, either. I finally thanked them for their time and Christie led me to another office with two desks. I had a brief chat with a client management rep named Veena, and then Andy – Michelle's son – who was working alongside Veena. They claimed they had no idea that Dennis had been doing anything wrong. We ended up in the kitchen, where Ben, Michelle's uncle, was eating lunch alone.

IN A LOWLY PLACE

"Hello," Ben said. He was a big man, sixty-ish, with thinning gray hair and a paunch. He stuffed the last of a Wendy's burger in his mouth, then talked around the bite. "My niece says you're looking into things with Dennis."

"That's correct."

Christie's gaze darted between Ben and me. "If you need me, I'll be up front." She looked quickly for her escape.

Ben watched her leave, then focused small eyes on me. "I hate to talk bad about Dennis, but he's been a handful. He's my nephew, and I like him, but ..." He wiped his hands on a napkin. "And as far as the blackmailing goes, I sure don't know anything." He sipped some Coke.

"That's what I'm hearing, but it seems like someone around here knew what he was doing." I looked at him curiously. "You've been with the company for how long?"

"Almost since its inception. Grant and I'll be passing along the operations to his kids in the next few years. I'm tired, and something like this situation with Dennis leaves a bad taste in my mouth." Another sip of Coke to emphasize that. "I don't have any kids, and I love my brother's kids, think of them as my own. To see one of them steal from us ..." He searched for words. "It's a shame."

"How much do you and Grant check the financials, the bids, and the bookkeeping?"

A small laugh. "Not as much as you might think. The kids handle a lot. I've done a lot of things around here, but I'm happy being the safety manager. I get to talk to the drivers, and I like that. I'm not in the office that much, and I go home at five every day. A boring life." He drained his drink and stood up. "It's been nice chatting with you, but I've got to get back to work."

I smiled as he threw his wrapper and paper cup in the trash, then stepped into the hall. He pointed to the main office.

"You take care."

I took my dismissal and headed out front. Christie barely glanced my way as I went outside. The hot sun hit me as I shielded my eyes and glanced around. Isaac was nowhere in sight, and the lot was quiet. So far, I wasn't coming up with any answers on who the blackmailer might've been, but I still had people to talk to, like Clyde Hessler and Warren Singletary.

It was lunchtime, and I stopped at a nearby Subway to get something to eat. While I ate my Baja chicken sub, I called Clyde Hessler. He didn't answer, so I left a message. By now, I was sure Michelle had talked to him. I hoped he wasn't avoiding me. Then I tried Taylor Walsh again, and it again went to voice mail. He probably didn't recognize the number and didn't answer. I thought about leaving a message, but what would I say? If I told him I was a private investigator, would he talk to me, even if I didn't say *why* I was calling? Or, *especially* if I didn't say why I was calling. I doubted it. Somehow I needed to talk to him. I realized I was faced with a dilemma. I needed to talk to Walsh, but I also needed to track down Warren Singletary and Clyde Hessler. I couldn't do all those things at the same time, so I decided to call for backup. I dialed a number and waited.

"Hey Reed, how are you?" Ace asked. He sounded sleepy, but then, with his languid way of speaking, he always did.

"I'm good," I said. We chatted for a minute, and then I said, "I need a favor, if you have time."

Ace's schedule varies, so I never know when he's at work. Deuce works in construction, every day from seven to four, and I knew he'd be busy now.

"You're in luck. It's my day off. What do you need?"

"I need to track down someone." I told him about this new investigation, how Taylor had been involved in the money drop, and how I needed to talk to Taylor Walsh. "Could you go to his apartment building and watch for him, and when he comes home report back to me?"

"Yeah, I could do that. But what if he goes out again?"

"Follow him," I said. "You've done that enough to know how to be careful, right?" I didn't know how well I'd trained him, but I'd also become more confident in both Ace and Deuce's judgment. "It'll be a big help."

"Yeah, you've trained me well." His tone was chagrined, and he was clearly holding something back.

"What's up?"

"Reed, don't you think I could do more? I know you don't want Deuce or me to do too much, or to screw things up, but give me a chance. If I see this guy, I could interview him and report back to you."

I stared out the window as I mulled that over. He was right. The Goofballs had done a lot for me over the years, and they were maturing in some important ways. Maybe it was time to take a chance. He cleared his throat, awaiting my reply. I made a decision. "You know what? If you see Walsh, talk to him, see what he tells you about the blackmail drop."

"Really?" He was so eager.

"Yes."

I spent a few minutes giving him more details of what I knew of Taylor Walsh, and coached him some on how to conduct an interview. I also texted him a link to Walsh's Facebook page, so he would know who to look for.

"Okay, Reed, you got it."

"Be careful, though. If this guy is involved in the blackmail scheme, he could be dangerous."

"I can handle myself."

"Yes, you can. Keep me posted as well, so I know where you are."

"No problem."

I thanked him and ended the call, then googled Warren Singletary. People-search sites have made it harder to find information – they all seem to want a fee for a full background check even if you only want an address – but I finally found one that listed his address for free. If the site was correct, he lived off Federal Boulevard, in south Denver. I finished my lunch and drove there. Singletary lived in a little tan bungalow off West Harvard Avenue, near Harvey Park. The houses had been built in the middle of the last century, and his was on a small lot with a detached one-car garage. A white SUV sat in the driveway. I parked across the street and watched the house for a moment. It was quiet. I finally got out and headed up the walk. I rang the bell twice and was about to conclude that Singletary wasn't home when a man in khaki shorts and a polo shirt answered. He pushed open a screen door.

"Yes?"

"Warren Singletary?" I asked.

"Yeah." He was suddenly cautious. "Who're you?"

I introduced myself and said, "I understand you used to work for Mowery Transportation?"

His cold green eyes narrowed. "Yes, I did. Why do you want to know?"

I didn't answer directly. "You knew Dennis Mowery, correct?"

"Not really." He surveyed me carefully. "We were in different departments. I hardly saw him."

I played puzzled. "That's interesting because I talked to Isaac Mowery, and he said he overheard you and Dennis arguing about something one time. Do you remember that incident?"

Singletary glanced over his shoulder, then shook his head. "I don't remember that, and I haven't seen Dennis in a long time. I hate to cut this short, but I'm working. I have a meeting in a few minutes, so I need to go."

I put a hand to the screen door. "Let me give you a business card, and maybe we can talk later." I used my other hand to reach for my wallet. I got out a card and handed it to him. He looked put out.

"Okay, Mister ..." He looked at the card. "Ferguson. But I doubt I'll have anything to say."

"Just in case," I said.

I didn't get a chance to say anything else as he backed up and shut the door. I let the screen door bang shut and slowly went down the walk, my suspicions aroused. Singletary didn't want to talk about his dispute with Dennis. Why?

I walked back to my car and drove around the block, then parked at the corner, where a big tree shielded my car. Through the tree branches, though, I could see Singletary's house. I waited and watched. I'd upset him, and at some point, he was going to act.

It was hot, but I didn't want to leave the engine running to draw attention to myself, so I rolled down a window and hunkered down. I turned on an '80s station and listened to The Smiths, The Psychedelic Furs, and Depeche Mode. I have a soft spot for that musical era. The afternoon dragged on, and I didn't see anything from Singletary's house. Some kids played in a yard down the block. I was sweating and growing tired. I texted Willie that I didn't know when I would be home and to eat dinner without me. I got a short reply several minutes later. I might've been reading too much into a text reply, but she didn't say what she'd do in my absence, or that she loved me, which she usually did. I made a mental note to ask her this evening. As long as I didn't get home too late.

Four o'clock. Then Singletary's front door opened and he emerged. He didn't look around, but went right to the SUV, got in, and drove down the street toward me. I ducked down and peeked over the dashboard. Singletary turned in my direction, so I quickly slumped over the seat. I heard the car go by, then I slowly raised my head and looked in the rearview mirror. The SUV was just turning the corner. I jammed the key in the ignition and started the 4-Runner, then followed. By the time I reached the corner, Singletary was a few blocks ahead. I tailed him, keeping a careful distance. He drove to Santa Fe Avenue, then north, and I kept pace. There was plenty of rush-hour traffic, but it was slow enough that I didn't have a problem staying with him. We headed into downtown, and I wondered where he was going. Was he heading to Mowery Transportation, maybe to confront Isaac? Once we got onto Seventeenth, I had a sneaky suspicion where he was going. Sure enough, he turned onto Larimer and pulled up near Step Recovery. A moment later, Dennis Mowery walked out of the building and up to the car. He got in, and the SUV drove off.

CHAPTER ELEVEN

What is going on? I thought as I watched Warren Singletary's SUV drive down the street. Dennis hadn't appeared to notice me. The street was packed with cars, and I kept a safe distance back as I followed. At one point, I thought I was going to lose Singletary at a stoplight, but then the SUV suddenly screeched to a halt before running the red light. I was several cars back. I tapped the steering wheel to "Dominion" by Sisters of Mercy. The light changed, and I stuck with the SUV as it drove south, and we eventually ended up at a large shopping center with a Walmart, a Hobby Lobby, and a strip of several other stores and restaurants. Singletary parked, and he and Dennis got out, crossed a street and walked into a Dazbog coffee shop. It was almost five o'clock. I pulled into a place farther away and pulled out binoculars from under my seat. Through the glass windows of the Dazbog, I vaguely made out Singletary and Dennis standing in line, and after paying for their orders, they came back outside. I tossed the binoculars on the passenger seat and hopped out. The two men found a table in the shade at the end of the building and sat down.

I watched them for a minute, wishing I could hear what they were saying. I quickly scoped things out and thought I might be able to hear their conversation if I sneaked down an alley and around the other

IN A LOWLY PLACE

side of the building. I started up the 4-Runner and moved to a different place, then got out again. I used the 4-Runner to shield me. Singletary and Dennis were still at the table, sipping their drinks. I dashed across the parking lot, then crossed the street and ran along the narrow alley between the buildings. When I got to the end, I peeked around the corner. Dennis and Singletary were nearby. They both had elbows on their table, deep in discussion. I eased back, leaned my shoulder against the side of the building, and strained my ears to listen.

"... telling you, we need to keep cool heads about us," Dennis was saying. "All this time has passed, and no one is going to find out about it now."

"How can you be so sure?" Singletary's voice shook with apprehension.

"Did anything happen then?" Dennis asked.

"... that detective ..."

Dennis said something inaudible.

"No, but what if someone did find out about it?" Singletary asked. "What if they come after you or me now? You never did know if ..."

I couldn't hear everything, and it was driving me nuts. There was too much noise from the roads and the shopping center.

"... did you say ..." Dennis's voice was too soft.

Singletary replied, but I missed it. Dennis said something else, and then, "I'll handle her."

I heard a noise behind me and glanced over my shoulder. A young woman in black slacks and a dark shirt had emerged from the building next door, carrying two large trash bags. She walked over to a dumpster and set the bags down, then opened one of the dumpster lids. It made a loud bang as she let it fall back. I swore to myself because I missed what Dennis said next.

Singletary then raised his voice a tad. "I don't like it."

"We covered our tracks."

Singletary didn't sound happy. "I don't know. I ..."

The woman shut the lid on the dumpster with another loud bang, and I didn't hear the rest of what he said. I glanced over my shoulder again and frowned at her, but in the dimness, she didn't even see me.

She went back into the restaurant, and I focused on Dennis and Singletary again.

"... would've been fine if Michelle hadn't gotten involved."

"What are you going to do about her?" Singletary asked.

"I'll see how it all plays out."

"... don't like it. It's too much pressure ..."

They talked a bit more, and I only caught snippets. Then my ears perked up.

"What about that detective?" Singletary swore. "He starts asking too many questions, what's he going to find?"

A large diesel pickup truck pulled into a parking place near the tables, the engine rumbling like a freight train. I swore silently again. Could I not catch a break? A man got out, but he kept the engine running. I stole a look and saw a woman in the passenger seat. It was hot, the windows were rolled up, and I figured she was enjoying the air conditioning while he ran into the coffee shop. But I couldn't hear a darn thing except for the consistent growl of the truck's engine. Singletary and Dennis were still talking, their heads close together now. I fumed, but there was nothing I could do. I waited and watched. The truck driver finally came out of the coffee shop and got back in the truck. I could see through the windshield as he handed the woman her drink, and he took a sip of his. After what seemed like an incredibly long time, the man finally put the truck in gear and pulled away from the coffee shop. A blessed silence ensued. Then I heard Dennis again.

"... good thing you're sober now. Can you imagine if we were trying to deal with all of this when we were drunk?"

"I kinda wish I was. Then I wouldn't be so scared."

Dennis laughed. "I'm telling you, you need to relax. I'll handle this, just like I did before."

"Yeah, I guess so." Singletary didn't sound convinced.

They talked for a few minutes more, nothing that I could discern as anything important, just some AA talk, and a little bit about Singletary's work, some kind of dispatch job. They soon got up and threw their cups in the trash. I raced back down the alley, hurried across the street, and got into the 4-Runner just as they appeared around the other side of the building. They got in the SUV and drove away. I stayed in hot pursuit, figuring that Singletary would be taking Dennis back downtown to Step Recovery. The SUV got on Santa Fe and headed north, confirming my suspicion. But then they surprised me when Singletary turned onto Alameda and drove east, past Broadway. I followed, and he turned into a nice neighborhood of older homes, many that had been renovated. Singletary parked in front of a large two-story house with a long, curved driveway. I parked behind a dark-colored car and watched them with my binoculars. They sat in the SUV and talked for a minute. Dennis waved his hand a time or two, and Singletary nodded. Then Dennis got out of the car and headed up the driveway. When he reached the porch, the door opened to reveal Michelle Farley. I had not expected that. I bit my lip. Why had Singletary dropped Dennis off here, rather than at Step Recovery? I glanced at my watch. Almost six o'clock. Maybe Dennis was there for dinner. He walked into the house, and the SUV drove off. I decided to keep tabs on Singletary. I knew where to find Dennis, and I could ask him and Michelle about his visit later.

The SUV turned right, and once it vanished, I sped down the street. I saw the car down the block and tailed it. Singletary drove south, and before long, he was back at his house. He parked in the driveway, ambled up the sidewalk, then let himself inside. I parked across the street and dashed to the front door. I didn't want to give him time to think, and I quickly rang the bell. A moment later, he opened the door and his jaw dropped.

"What're you doing here?" he asked.

"You had a nice chat with Dennis," I said, daring him to lie.

"What? I don't ..." It was amusing to see him struggling for words. "This is crazy. I don't know what you're talking about. I –"

"Don't lie to me," I interrupted. "I saw you with him."

"You followed me?" A long string of curse words followed. "You had no right to do that."

I shrugged. "It's a free country. Want to tell me what you were talking about? You told me you hadn't seen Dennis in a long time."

His jaw worked as he tried to come up with something. He finally repeated, "I don't know what you're talking about." Not the best improvisational lying I've ever heard.

He started to shut the door, but I quickly yanked open the screen and put my hand out. "What are you worried about? What happened back when you both worked at Mowery?"

"Man, leave me alone or I'm going to call the police."

He put some force into the door and pushed it shut. I stood there for a moment, angry that I might not have handled that as well as I could have. I didn't get anything else from him.

I let the screen bang shut, then left Singletary's house and drove back by the Farley house. I didn't see Michelle or Dennis. I watched from down the street, but had no idea if they were there or had left. However, I knew where Dennis would have to go eventually, so I drove back downtown. I parked on Larimer Street and watched Step Recovery. While I waited, I called Cal. I hadn't heard from him about his research on the Mowerys. He didn't answer. I didn't bother with a message because I knew he'd call back when he could. Then I texted Ace for an update. I didn't get a reply, which had me a little worried. He'd said he was up to the task, but what if something went wrong? I couldn't imagine having to live with that knowledge. After a few minutes, I texted again, asking if he was okay. Still no reply. I ran a hand over my face as I questioned whether I'd done the right thing involving Ace in my work. But surely he could handle himself. Couldn't he?

My worry hadn't abated when I saw a black Escalade pull up in front of Step Recovery. A few men who were ambling around outside gave the car a good once-over. A moment later, the passenger door opened and Dennis Mowery got out.

CHAPTER TWELVE

I watched Dennis go into Step Recovery. Michelle's Escalade eased into traffic. I didn't think either one noticed my 4-Runner. I waited until the Escalade turned the corner, and then I got out and walked back to Step Recovery. A few men loitering near the entrance eyed me as I walked inside the lobby. Cool air hit me as I approached the counter. A grizzled older man with long hair was talking to another man in jeans and a tee shirt, and they both looked up at me when I approached.

"I'd like to talk to Dennis Mowery," I said.

The older man smiled politely as he exchanged a look with the other man.

"We don't give out the information of our residents," the grizzled man behind the counter said. "We have people coming and going throughout the week, and I can give him a message if he shows up."

I glared at him. "I know he's here."

He was unflappable, trained in the art of giving a blank look. I finally shrugged and went outside. Several men ambled near the main entrance, a few more near a side door to Step Recovery. I walked partway down the block, then pulled out my phone and called Dennis. No answer. I left him a message to call me and pocketed my phone. I paced up and down and waited for a reply. Then the grizzled man walked out of Step Recovery. I hurried farther down the block before he saw me. I passed two men in faded jeans and wrinkled shirts as I ducked into the alley and looked back.

"Hey, how are you two doing tonight?" I heard the grizzled man say to the two men.

"How ya doin', Lou?" one of the men replied.

"Chapel services tonight," Lou said.

"Yeah, we might come in." This voice was gruff and phlegmy.

"It's a nice way to get out of the heat," Lou went on. "And if you want to stay for the AA meeting after, you can. We'll have cookies, coffee, and some sandwiches."

"We'll see," the gruff voice said.

"All right, you take care," Lou said.

I peeked around the corner. Lou was headed in the other direction to talk to a couple of other men hanging around.

"I just want to get something to eat," the first man said as he hefted up his jeans.

"Yeah," the other one said. "We know the schtick, and so does Lou."

"He has to try."

They laughed and walked slowly toward the open side door. Lou was still down the street, engaged in another conversation. I quickly stepped behind the two men and slipped through the door with them. The room we entered was large, with a small carpeted platform at one end, a large wooden cross hung on the wall behind it. At the opposite end were double doors that led into Step Recovery. Rows of plastic chairs were set up, and several men were already seated. A man with a Bible was talking to some of them. The two men went to a row in the middle, but I took a seat near the back, away from the side door. The man with the Bible came over and asked me how I was doing as he shook my hand. I told him fine, and we engaged in small talk for a moment. He had a pleasant manner about him, warm and inviting. He saw a few men that he seemed to know and waved at them, then courteously moved on. I soon saw Lou enter through the side door with one of the men he'd been talking to outside, and I turned away. Lou took a seat up front.

A few minutes before eight, Dennis walked in through the double doors. He glanced around, and I made sure to make eye contact. His mouth opened, and he looked to the side door, then seemed to think better of running. I smiled broadly at him and gestured for him to join me. He approached me as if he were walking the plank, then sat down next to me and stared straight ahead.

"What're you doing here?" he hissed.

"I needed to talk to you. I left you a message and you didn't call back."

He felt in his pocket. "I didn't hear the phone ring."

I got to the point. "You've been a busy man – work, and then meeting up with Warren Singletary."

His face went white. "I don't know what you're talking about," he finally managed to say. He was no better a liar than Singletary.

It was now eight o'clock, and the chaplain went to the front and stood on the platform. He raised a hand to quiet everyone. "Thank you all for joining us tonight," he said, an easiness about him. "What a blessed and beautiful evening we have."

"You're not a well-liked man," I said in a low voice to Dennis. He stared at the chaplain and didn't reply. I went on. "I've talked to a lot of people about you today, and they paint a different picture of you than you do of yourself. Or that Michelle does, either."

His spine stiffened. "What do you mean?"

"What are you and Singletary up to?"

"Nothing." The reply was quick and irritated.

The chaplain was talking, and a man in the next row swiveled in his seat and glowered at us. He mouthed for us to pipe down.

Dennis whispered an apology, then murmured to me, "We can't talk about this now." He nodded toward the front. "After."

I wanted to tell him to step outside now, but I knew he wouldn't do that. Instead, we stayed and listened to the chaplain for about thirty minutes. Everyone sang "A Mighty Fortress Is Our God," and he read from the Gospel of John, gave a short sermon about accountability, and at the end, we all stood up and sang "Amazing Grace." It was a pleasant service, but it also gave Dennis time to think through his responses, and to craft some possible lies. I was edgy as we finished with "The Old Rugged Cross," and as we sang the last line, I pointed to the side door.

"Let's go talk," I said to Dennis.

He glanced around nervously and avoided curious stares. The room was a cacophony of noises as several men slid the plastic chairs around and arranged them in a large oval for the AA meeting. Some of the people left through both doors, and others went to a long table where sandwiches were being set out. Dennis and I stepped outside, where it was quieter. Dusk had turned everything into shadows, but it was still warm. He wiped the sweat off his brow and gestured for me to follow him. He hurried to the end of the block and around the corner, then stopped and whirled on me. He raised a hand in a flash of anger, then dropped it.

"Have you been following me?"

I didn't reply to that. "I've been doing a lot of digging today. You're not a popular guy."

He crossed his arms. "What's that supposed to mean?"

I ticked things off with my fingers. "I talked to Kim, and she says that your marriage wasn't very good, that you might've cheated on her, and that you have a violent streak."

"That's not true," he said. "I never hit her, and I didn't cheat on her. We got along fine until I began drinking and drugging."

I widened my eyes skeptically. "Are you sure you want to stick with that?"

He fumed for a moment. "Maybe we fought other times, but I never cheated on her."

"So when you came home late, or not at all, it was because you were sleeping at the office?"

"Yes." I tended to believe that. He fumed. "Regardless, what does this have to do with someone blackmailing me?"

"I can't see your ex having a motive to blackmail you, but why do the two of you have such differing views of your marriage?"

"She's lying."

"Or maybe you are."

Something flickered in his eyes, but he wisely stayed quiet. A couple of hard-looking guys walked past us, and they glanced at Dennis. He turned away from them.

"I hear you're not well-liked at Step," I said.

"How would you know? We're supposed to have anonymity."

"Some people like to talk." He swore, and I went on. "They say you like to blame others, that I should be wary of you."

"They don't need to know about my life."

"What're you hiding? Someone overheard you talking about keeping quiet."

His mouth worked. "I'm not hiding anything."

He was such a bad liar. "I've been talking to people at Mowery Transportation as well. No one came out and said it, but it doesn't sound like you were very well-liked there, either."

He shrugged. "So what? I don't have to be liked to do my job. And they don't at Step, either."

"True." I contemplated him for a moment. "What went on between you and Isaac over the years?"

He didn't try to hide his scorn. "Isaacs's the baby of the family, and he always got treated better. We're just two very different people."

"That sounds like a pat answer. Want to tell me the truth?"

He watched cars drive by for a minute. "He's always thought he was better than me. He's got a chip on his shoulder, thinks I look down on him because he'd rather be working with the guys in the warehouse than in an office. I couldn't care less." He frowned. "And I know he was frustrated about my drinking. He would get mad when he suspected I was drinking or high at work."

I was getting impatient with his answers. "Can you blame them?"

He hung his head. "No, I guess not."

"Isaac wasn't the only one who thought you were drinking on the job." I tapped him on the shoulder so he would look at me, then I locked eyes with him. "Do you realize if you slipped up and talked about stealing from the company, someone could've heard you." His lips were a thin line." Did you ever tell Isaac what was going on?"

He shook his head halfheartedly. "No."

"You don't know for sure, do you?"

He suddenly looked forlorn. "I don't know. So much of that time is a blur. But Isaac wouldn't blackmail me."

"No, but there was something going on between you, Isaac, and Warren Singletary. What was that about?"

His gaze darted around. "It was no big deal."

I ran a hand slowly over my face, trying not to let my anger get the best of me. "If you want me to help you, you need to tell me what's going on. The argument didn't sound like' no big deal' to Isaac. And I know it's a big deal to you and Singletary. I overheard you talking about it. Singletary's scared."

"You were following me."

We were back to that. I shook my head. "No, I was following Singletary, and he led me to you."

He opened his mouth to say something, then clamped it shut. He watched the street again, gears churning in his mind. "Warren had a drinking problem, too. He would come to work drunk. You can't be doing that if you're working with the trucks. He could lose his CDL license."

I wasn't buying it. There was more than he was telling me. I waited as a Corvette raced by, then said, "I'm going to look into this. If you're lying to me, I will find out."

He worked hard to make eye contact with me. "It's the truth."

"Why wouldn't Singletary tell me about the drinking?"

"Because it would've gotten us both into trouble. I knew about his drinking, and I should've reported it."

"Even though you were drinking?" I said sarcastically.

"I still should've reported him."

A bad feeling washed over me, as if I were being watched. I peered into the growing darkness, but didn't see anyone paying attention to Dennis and me. I brushed aside my apprehension. "Are you telling me the truth?"

He looked at me uneasily. "Yes."

"Is there anything you're not telling me about the blackmailing? I can't help you if you don't tell me everything."

"It's exactly as I told you."

"I've been able to track down the waiter, Taylor. I'm going to talk to him to see if he can shed light on the blackmail drop and who he gave the money to."

He sighed with relief. "Good. You'll find out I'm not lying about any of that."

"We'll see," I murmured.

He jabbed a finger at me. "I'm telling you the truth."

"You understand why that's hard for me to believe when you've lied about other things."

"Just Warren," he said sheepishly. "That was a mistake, okay?"

"Why'd you meet him today?"

"It was nothing."

"Dennis, what's going on between you and Singletary?"

"You can let that go," he snapped. "All I want to know is who was blackmailing me."

I wasn't going to let anything go between him and Singletary, but I didn't tell Dennis that. His jaw was tight, and I knew he wasn't going to say anything else about Singletary. I went on. "You're friends with John Talbot?"

"Not anymore."

"You have his number, though? I'd like to talk to him."

He hesitated. "Man, it's been a while. Let me think." He pondered for a moment, then gave me a number. "I think that's it. You can talk to him, but I don't know what you'll find." He took out his phone and glanced at it. "I need to get back. We can talk more tomorrow, okay?"

I nodded, and we started walking to the corner. Then he hesitated.

"How about I walk back now, and you go later?"

I wasn't sure why he didn't want to be seen with me, but I nodded. I stayed at the corner as he hurried back to Step Recovery and walked in the main door. As I headed to my car, my mind raced.

There was more to this blackmail plot than met the eye.

CHAPTER THIRTEEN

I still couldn't shake the feeling someone was watching me, so I sat in the 4-Runner for a minute and stared out at Larimer Street. The traffic was lighter, and several people walked up and down the block, but I didn't see anyone that I thought acted suspiciously. I checked the alley entrances as well, but saw no one lurking. I finally started the car and drove down Larimer and the surrounding blocks, then finally concluded I was losing my mind. I wasn't far from the condo, and was about to call Willie when Ace called me.

"Hey, Reed."

"Ace, I've been trying to get hold of you."

"I saw you called, but Deuce and I were talking to that guy, Taylor."

"Wait, Deuce was with you?"

"Yeah. We're heading to B 52s now. Why don't you meet us there and we can tell you what happened?"

"I'm not far from there, so I'll see you in a few."

"Okay."

I ended the call and tried Willie but she didn't answer. I left her a message and invited her to join us, then drove the few blocks to B 52s.

When I got to B 52's, Ace and Deuce were playing pool at a table in a back room. B 52's is a pool hall in a converted warehouse, and I love the place. It's decorated with airplane propellers and advertisements from the '40s, but they play '80s music, which I enjoy, although admittedly, it has nothing to do with the World War II era. As I walked up to Ace and Deuce, I got a text from Willie that said she wasn't home yet and to have a good time, that she'd see me soon. That was odd. Normally she'd tell me where she was.

"Hey, Reed, what's wrong?" Deuce asked.

I stared at my phone for a moment. "Willie won't be joining us." I puzzled on that. She hadn't mentioned working overtime, so where was she? "I don't know, guys, but there's something off with her."

"Oh," Ace said. "Is everything okay?"

"I'm not sure." I put my phone in my pocket. "I probably should wrap this up soon and get home."

Ace put down his pool cue. "We have a table here, and we ordered you a Fat Tire."

"Great." I like brown ales, such as Fat Tire, because they're less bitter, and although I'll try something new now and again, I always gravitate to Fat Tire. I took a drink and said, "Deuce, how did you end up helping Ace?"

Deuce set aside his cue stick and they eagerly sat down at the table.

"I went to Taylor Walsh's apartment, like you said," Ace began. "It was boring for a while because nothing happened. I played some games on my phone, but even that got boring. I don't know how you do surveillance and not lose your mind."

"A hazard of the job," I murmured.

Ace looked at me as if he didn't quite understand what I meant, but he went on. "It got to be four o'clock, and Deuce called me ..."

"Because that's when I get off work," Deuce said. "And I was wondering what he was doing, so –"

"I told him," Ace continued. "I remembered what you said, Reed, about how if I talked to Taylor, it could be dangerous –"

"So he asked me to come and be his backup," Deuce finished.

I sipped my beer and listened as they told their tale.

"So Deuce came over, and he watched with me," Ace said. "You sent me Walsh's Facebook page –"

"So we knew what he looked like," Deuce interjected. "And we were both watching for him, and I was watching Ace's car."

I smiled. "Good." I sat back, sipped my beer, and listened.

"Walsh finally came home around six o'clock," Ace said.

"I saw him first," Deuce clarified. "He drove past my truck in a beat-up SUV, and I recognized him. He parked around the side of his building."

Ace bobbed his head excitedly. "Yeah, so I waited until he walked upstairs. I saw him go into his apartment, and I went up to talk to him."

"And I watched from down the walkway, but I could hear him," Deuce said. "We didn't want to scare him, so –"

"We agreed Deuce should stay out of sight, but he'd be there in case something happened," Ace said. "And I knew I wouldn't go inside, no matter what. I knocked on the door, and Walsh answered right away. I introduced myself and asked if he was Taylor Walsh. He said yes, but then he asked me who I was and why I wanted to know. I said a friend told me Taylor might be able to help me. I think he thought I was wanting to buy some drugs, so I just let him go on thinking that. Then I noticed a couple of ski posters on the walls, and a set of skis in the corner, so I asked him about skiing."

"We've heard you talk about how you try to be nice to someone so that they don't get suspicious of your questions," Deuce said.

Ace nodded. "How you talk about something they like, to take them off guard and keep them talking."

"He was getting suspicious," Deuce explained.

I suppressed a smile and looked at them. They'd observed more than I realized, I thought. Good for them.

Ace sipped his beer and went on. "I told Walsh I liked to ski at Loveland, and he chatted with me for a bit about that. Sounds like he's a wicked good skier; he talked about skiing Wild Child and some other double black diamond runs."

"Yeah, Ace and I did some when we were younger, but not anymore."

"You remember 9 Lives at Breck?" Ace said to Deuce. "We had to hike fifteen minutes to it, then I about wiped out."

"It was funny," Deuce laughed. "You were yelling at me to shut up and –"

"Guys," I said to focus them.

"Oh, right." Ace blushed. "Anyway, if Walsh skis double black diamonds, he's good."

"Or crazy," Deuce interjected.

"Right." Ace nodded. "I didn't want to ask Walsh right away about what he knew about the blackmail stuff so I just said something about him working at Billy's on Broadway."

"And Walsh said he did," Deuce said.

"Yes, but then he told me he now works at Blazing Bistro." Ace grinned. "I think he told me because we were talking about skiing, and he was kinda relaxed."

Deuce looked at me seriously. "That's helpful for you, right?"

I nodded. "Yes, that is. What else happened?"

Ace took another drink and continued. "I tried to keep it light, friendly, so I said that I was helping out a friend. Now I figured I'd ask what I wanted to, and could he tell me about the time he took an envelope and passed it on to somebody. At that point he got mad and said he didn't have to talk to me. And then he –"

"Slammed the door in Ace's face," Deuce said.

"Well," I said, slightly disappointed, "that's not bad, though. You got where he works now."

Deuce shook his head excitedly. "It doesn't end there, Reed, because then –"

"We went back to our cars," Ace said, "but we didn't leave. We decided to see what Walsh would do. We waited a while, and sure enough, he came back out of his apartment. It was about that time that you texted me, so I couldn't answer –"

"But we'd agreed that we would talk to Walsh again," Deuce said, "but I'd be along, like the muscle."

"You know, to scare him," Ace said.

Deuce was solid, but he was so nice and friendly, I had a hard time seeing how he might intimidate anyone.

Deuce smiled grimly. "We watched Walsh as he walked to his car in the parking lot, and then both Ace and I approached him."

"Don't worry, we wouldn't have done anything to him," Ace said gravely.

"I know," I said. "Go on."

"Walsh was shocked to see us," Ace said, "and he cussed us out. But we acted kind of tough, and I told him that he needed to talk to me or I would go to the police. At that point –"

"He told us not to do that, but he still wasn't talking," Deuce said. "I stepped up to him, and he caved. All I did was stand there and flex my muscles." He grinned.

"I told him what you told me Reed, about taking money from your client and passing it to someone else, and I accused him of being part of a blackmail scheme," Ace said. "He said he didn't know anything about that, that all that happened was he got a text asking if he wanted to make some extra money. When he found out how much – five hundred – he figured it was worth asking about. Walsh said money's always tight, and he was going to listen. I asked him if he thought it could've been something to do with drugs, and he wasn't too worried about that. Anyway, he said yes, and he got a text telling him what to do. It said a man would come into the restaurant, I think he said on a Thursday, and sit in Walsh's section. He'd leave an envelope, and all Walsh had to do was take it and leave it on some crates near a dumpster in the alley. Then Walsh should go back into the restaurant, and then he was supposed to check the crates later, and there'd be an envelope with the five hundred bucks for him. The text also said Walsh would be watched, and he better not try anything fishy. Walsh asked us why he wouldn't do something like that. He said it was easy money, and he wanted to buy some new skis."

"Did you ask him if he worried that what he was doing might be illegal?" I asked.

"I did," Ace said proudly. "Walsh brushed that off and said it didn't matter to him. What'd he say? Oh yeah, that people do stuff all the time. He didn't care about that, and he could use the money."

"So he did as instructed," Deuce continued the story, "and when the guy showed up with the envelope, Walsh took it. After he'd taken the guy's order, he went back outside and hid the envelope in the crates. Then he went back inside and went back to work."

"Except the last time," Ace said. "Walsh said he stayed and watched from the kitchen window and saw someone take the envelope, then put a different one on the crate."

"Any idea who that was? What did he look like?" I asked.

"We asked him that, too," Ace said. "He said the guy wore a dark hoodie and dark sunglasses –"

"And jeans," Deuce added.

Ace nodded. "He was about six-foot and thinner. Walsh said he waited a second, then went into the alley and peeked around the dumpster. He thought it was a guy, but it could've been a tall woman. Whoever it was walked down the alley and left."

"We even asked Walsh if he saw anything unusual about the person," Deuce said. "But he didn't."

I thought about that for a moment. "All three times, passing the money happened the same way?"

"Yes, except the last time where Walsh watched for the blackmailer," Deuce said.

I then remembered what Dennis had told me about that last transaction. "The last time, my client left the bar and went around to the alley to try to see what was going on, but he got waylaid, and by the time he got there, all he saw was Walsh smoking a cigarette."

Ace nodded. "Yes, Walsh said he used a smoking break so that he could go outside to pass the envelope along."

I twirled my beer bottle in my hand. "Did Walsh say what he thought when he was asked to help the second and third times?" I asked.

"He acted like it wasn't any big deal." Deuce scratched his chin. "Or, maybe he was a little nervous the third time, but it was still five hundred bucks."

"Did he see anything else noteworthy?" I asked.

Both brothers shook their heads.

"No, not that he told us anyway," Deuce said.

"Did we do good?" Ace asked.

I smiled at them. "Yeah, good work, guys."

"At least now, you know where Walsh works," Deuce said. "If he isn't home, you could go to his work to talk to him there."

"You're right, that helped. You two did great," I said. I glanced at my watch. "I hate to do this, but I really should get home. I need to check on Willie." I got out some money and put it on the table. "This is on me, and I'll also cut you guys a check. You've earned it."

"Wow, that's awesome," Ace said. "It was fun, and if you need more help –"

"You let us know." Deuce nodded at me.

I thanked them both again and got up to leave. It was nice to see the Goofballs so happy, and I had to admit that I was pleasantly surprised. They'd handled the surveillance and interview well, and I would've probably made some of the same decisions that they did. They'd gotten some good information from Taylor Walsh, and they hadn't gotten hurt in the process. I couldn't ask for more.

CHAPTER FOURTEEN

When I got home, Willie was sitting in front of the TV with Humphrey on her lap.

"Hey, hon, I'm sorry I'm late," I said.

She nodded, and her eyes stayed on the TV. I looked at her, then at Humphrey, who popped his head up, then went back to sleeping. An old *Friends* episode was on TV.

"Where were you?" I asked. "You didn't mention having to work later."

She finally looked at me. "No. I was with Darcy."

"Oh? How is Darcy?"

"She's fine." Willie glanced out the window.

Darcy Cranston lives across the street in one of three apartments carved out of an old Victorian house that Willie and I own. Willie's been friends with Darcy since they both lived in the building, before Willie moved in with me. Darcy's a hoot to be with, and I would've thought she could've boosted Willie's mood, but that didn't seem to be the case.

I walked over and purposely blocked her view of the TV so she would have to look at me. "Darcy's fine, but you're not. What's going on?"

She drew in a breath and sighed heavily. Then she patted the seat next to her. "Why don't you sit down?"

Good Lord, there's nothing worse than hearing that. I was in some kind of trouble. I plodded over to the couch, my mind racing with all the things I must've done but that I couldn't think of right now. I made it to the couch and sat down next to her. Then I waited expectantly.

"Sorry I haven't been saying a whole lot lately," she began. "I know you probably think you did something."

She knew me too well. I had been focused on me. A wave of guilt washed over me, and I focused on her. "What's going on?"

She took a moment. "I haven't told you yet, but I found a lump on my breast. It's got me scared. I went over to talk to Darcy about it, but I haven't told anyone else yet, not even my family. I don't know why I haven't wanted to talk to you. I guess if I talk to you about it, then it's real. And I don't want this to be real."

I took her hand in mine and ignored the thumping in my chest. Her talking about it made it real. What was going on, and what if it was serious? I sat for a moment.

"I had a mammogram the other day, and they didn't like the results. They now want me to have a diagnostic mammogram on Friday, and if it's ... serious ... well, we'll have to see what happens," she said. "If the second mammogram results are positive, I'll have to have a biopsy. If that's the case, would you go with me for that?"

"Of course," I said. She petted Humphrey and didn't say anything. "Whatever is happening, we'll deal with it together," I finally said. "But let's not put the cart before the horse. It could be nothing. Let's see what happens with the second mammogram."

She nodded slowly. "I keep telling myself the same thing, but then my mind races ahead, does all of the what-ifs. It's scary."

I nodded and pulled her close. Humphrey gave a little meow, then hopped off her lap and settled on the arm of the couch.

"Don't get carried away. Let's just see what happens next. Then we'll go from there. It's going to be okay," I said, mustering as much rational, level-headed thinking as I could. But, to tell the truth, I was as concerned as she was.

The next morning, as Willie and I both got ready for work, she seemed a little more chipper. I'm sure her health had been a heavy burden for her to carry around, and I hoped that telling me about it had made her feel a tiny bit better. Once she was off to work, I fed Humphrey, then called John Talbot, using the number Dennis had supplied for his best friend, hoping Dennis had remembered it correctly. It was the right number, but Talbot didn't answer, so I left a message, briefly explaining that Dennis had given me his number and asking him to call me. Then I headed for Mowery Transportation. I'd never heard from the office manager, Clyde Hessler, and I hoped he would be there today.

I got to Mowery shortly before nine, and Christie Costa greeted me with a cool smile before leading me to a large corner office, where Grant Mowery sat behind a huge mahogany desk. Behind him were bookcases displaying some awards, a few business books, and several truck models. Another wall held a few framed photos of him standing in front of big rigs with the company logo on them. A window opposite looked out toward Interstate 70. Grant got up and approached me.

"You're Reed Ferguson." He walked around the desk and extended a big hand. His grip was firm. "Take a seat."

I sat across from him in a comfortable leather chair, and I felt dwarfed by both the desk and his presence. Like his brother Ben, Grant was a big man, but where Ben seemed soft, Grant still looked as if he could play linebacker. His dark eyes took me in.

"Helluva thing we have going on here," he said as he put his fingertips together. "I can't tell you how upsetting it was to hear what Dennis had done. I was disappointed, for sure. I wish that darn kid would get things together. It's difficult to watch your kids struggle in any way, but watching him piss his life away with drinking and drugs, well, I can't even begin to tell you what that's like."

He was feeding me answers without my having to ask. All I said was, "Oh?" And he went on. My mind momentarily wandered to Willie, and I had to tell myself to focus.

Grant ran a hand through a thicket of gray hair. "When I started this company, I always figured I'd be able to pass it along to our kids.

And Ben invested, but he didn't end up having any kids, and he treats mine as if they were his." He smiled. "Which is great. You want to have your family around you. That's important." I nodded. "I've been so pleased that my three kids have wanted to be involved in the company." He waved a hand in the air. "Oh, sure, they all went off to college and did their own thing for a while, to get themselves seasoned, but they've all come back here." He tapped the desk with a finger. "It's a good operation, though. It would be attractive employment for anybody, not just my kids." He leaned forward. "I'm not bragging, mind you, but we've done well here. We operate in several states, and we've won awards. We know what we're doing."

"I see," I said. My phone buzzed but I ignored it.

"I would have never thought Dennis would get himself into any trouble. Michelle and Isaac never did. Dennis is blaming it on his knee surgery, that he got hooked on painkillers at that time. I suppose that's possible, but he had everything going for him. You would've thought he would get some help." He paused and glanced out the window for a moment. "I had no idea he was stealing from us, though. I mean, I look at the accounts now and again, but I'm at an age where I'm beginning to offload a lot to the kids. They're handling things. Well, at least I assumed they had everything under control." He locked eyes with me. "I suppose that was naïve on my part, but that's where I was at."

A knock on the door interrupted us, and Grant said in a booming voice, "Come in."

I swiveled in my chair to see Ben Mowery standing in the doorway. He took a couple of tentative steps into the room and squinted at me.

"Sorry, I didn't know you were busy," Ben said.

Grant shrugged that off. "It's not a big deal. What's going on?"

Ben took a few more steps toward the desk. "I was going to talk to you about that new safety qualification. We have to get up to speed on that. But we can discuss it another time."

Grant quickly consulted a desk calendar. "How about lunch?"

Ben glanced at me again. "Sure. I'll come back later."

Grant nodded, and Ben backed out of the room and closed the door. Grant stared at the door for moment.

"He's been acting a little strange lately. I think he's got some health issues." He raised an eyebrow at me. "Did he tell you about that?"

I shook my head. "We didn't talk for very long."

"He's not one for words. We don't see him in the office much. He'll come in for lunch, tends to eat by himself in the cafeteria. I'm a little surprised he agreed to go to lunch with me." He laughed. "I suppose I'm the one who takes more advantage of being the top dog around here. Ben has always been quiet, likes to be out there with the drivers and all the machinery. You hardly see him around the office." Then he frowned. "Maybe I shouldn't have told you about his health issues."

I kept a straight face, thinking about Willie. "It's okay, I won't say anything."

He went on without missing a beat. "When all this stuff came up with Dennis, Ben and I talked about it. Besides being stunned, neither of us noticed any irregularities. I'm glad we let Dennis go when we did, although this whole blackmailing thing just makes me sick. I can't believe all this is happening at this company."

"Whose idea was it to let him go?"

"Mine."

For the first time, I wondered if he wasn't being entirely truthful. I remembered how Kim Mowery and Isaac had said that Michelle had been the force behind Dennis's firing, not Grant.

He looked at me with hard dark eyes. "I do hope you find whoever blackmailed Dennis. I guess he told Michelle he wants to know who it was so he can put the whole thing behind him, but I'd like to put that person in jail. They shouldn't be doing that when someone's struggling with an issue. You don't kick people when they're down." A deep breath as he got pensive. The office was quiet. "I know the kids think we treated Isaac the best, and Dennis and Isaac have their disagreements, but I don't know what that's all about. As far as my wife and I are concerned, we treated them the same. Dennis was quiet, not into football or things like that like Isaac was. Sure, we went to all of Isaac's football games, supported him with his sports, but that didn't mean we liked him or treated him better than Dennis. Or Michelle. Do you have siblings?"

I shook my head. "No, it's just me."

"I've heard that that can be a blessing, although I can't imagine growing up without a sibling. Ben and I get along well, always have. It was logical for us to be in business together, although neither one of us pictured it getting this big. But it's been nice. We'll both be able to enjoy our retirements, let the kids take things over."

I finally asked another question. "Do you have any idea who might have known that Dennis was stealing from the company, or who might've blackmailed him?"

He leaned back. "I've been thinking about that since I found out about this whole thing, and the answer is no. We employ a lot of people at Mowery, and I suppose anybody could have figured it out. I've got access to the books, Ben does, and our office manager, Clyde Hessler. Along with Michelle and Isaac. None of us caught what Dennis was doing, though. And he could have been manipulating the contracts as well. And Dennis admits to being in a haze – that's what he calls it – while he worked here. He could've told somebody." His eyes narrowed. "I just gave you a number of suspects, but let me tell you, I don't see any of them blackmailing Dennis."

You may be right, I thought to myself, but someone had to have known what was going on. The problem was, I wasn't finding who that was.

"Well, this has been a nice conversation," he said. "But I do have a few things I need to attend to. Is there anything else you need from me?"

I stood up. "Not at the moment. Thank you for your time."

Grant had done all the talking, had controlled the interview, but he'd also answered all the questions I might've asked. I thanked him for his time and left.

CHAPTER FIFTEEN

When I reached the reception area, Christie Costa signaled to me.

"Michelle wants to talk to you," she said. "She said she called you on your cell phone."

I pulled my phone from my pocket. Sure enough, the call that I'd missed when I was talking to Grant Mowery was from Michelle, but she hadn't left a message. I smiled at Christie.

"She's not here?"

Christie shook her head. "No, she didn't come in."

"I'll call her back. Is Clyde Hessler here?"

"Not yet," she said, then quickly picked up the phone so she wouldn't have to talk to me.

I thanked her and stepped outside. The sounds of trucks and cars were loud in the parking lot and nearby streets, so I got into my car and called Michelle.

"Reed, I need to talk to you. It's Dennis. Someone beat him up last night."

"What? I left him at Step Recovery about nine, and I thought he'd gone back inside the building."

"He told me you two had talked, but after that, he went out again and someone attacked him. He didn't even let me know until this morning. I picked him up and brought him to my house. Could you come over?"

She gave me the address. I knew where she lived, but I didn't tell her that.

"I'll be there soon," I said.

I was walking up the long driveway to Michelle Farley's front door when a black truck pulled into the driveway. A man in tan slacks and a short-sleeved black shirt got out. He was on the thin side, about my height, and clean-shaven.

"You must be Reed Ferguson, the detective," he said. "I'm Roger Farley. Michelle said you'd be stopping by."

I was tempted to correct him and tell him I was a "private investigator," much as the lead character used to do in *Magnum PI*, an old television series. Somehow "detective" sounded a tad insulting coming from Farley, but I let it go. I shook his hand, and he gestured toward the house.

"Michelle was almost hysterical when she found out what happened to Dennis." His tone was tempered, but a lack of fondness for Dennis was evident.

I studied him carefully. "You don't like Dennis?"

He paused at the screen door, but didn't open it. I could see shadows in the hallway behind him. "Between you and me, not really," he said in a low voice. "Michelle dotes on her brothers, but I don't see it. And when one was stealing from the company, it's hard to forgive that, don't you think?"

I shrugged. "It's not really for me to say."

"Well, I'll say it. It wasn't cool." His brow creased. "And Isaac has always rubbed me the wrong way. He thinks he's smarter than everyone else. I don't need that."

"You work at Mowery Transportation?"

"Yeah, I'm a lackey," he said, then quickly went on. "Eh, actually, I'm the Senior Operations Manager at Mowery Transportation. I oversee most of the departments." His eyes crinkled with lines of disappointment. "I was going to start my own company, selling parts for foreign cars. But Michelle thought I'd make more money if I joined their business. And she talked me into it." He surveyed me. "Are you on your own, or do you work for someone else?"

"I'm on my own," I said.

"You're lucky."

I puzzled as to why he was telling me all this, but since he wanted to talk, I'd keep listening and get what I could from him.

"Grant offered me a position at Mowery Transportation a long time ago, but I didn't want to take it. I didn't want to have to answer to them," he said. I sensed a rivalry between Roger and his in-laws, but I kept quiet. "And now they've got our son Andy working there, and Michelle wants our other son, Jordan, to work there, too. I don't know how I feel about that. I think I'd rather my kids work somewhere else."

He didn't get to say more because Michelle materialized in the hall behind him and opened the screen door.

"What are you two doing out here?" She stared at her husband. "Let the man in."

Roger stepped aside to let me in. "How's Dennis doing?"

I couldn't tell if Michelle noticed the tone, but I certainly did.

"He's fortunate it wasn't worse," she said. She didn't seem as upset as I thought she'd be. "I tried to get him to go to the ER, but he refused. I even told him I'd take care of the bill."

"Of course you did," Roger muttered.

"What was that?" she asked.

"Nothing." He subtly rolled his eyes at me. "Where's Dennis now?"

"He's on the back porch," she said. "I can't believe someone assaulted him. Does this have something to do with the blackmail?"

Roger shrugged. "I highly doubt it. That happened a long time ago. Dennis was probably at the wrong place at the wrong time. Let's get a cup of coffee and calm down."

She nodded and looked at me. "I'll bet Dennis would like to talk to Reed in private. Are you okay with that?"

"Sure," I said.

She waved a hand for me to follow. "Coffee?" she called over her shoulder.

I declined.

Roger frowned. "I'd like to hear what Dennis has to say."

We walked into the kitchen, and Michelle pointed to sliding doors. "Dennis is out there."

She tapped Roger's arm and poured him a cup of coffee. I thanked her, ignored another eyeroll from Roger, and stepped outside. Dennis sat in a lounge chair in jeans and a blue tee shirt. He was staring into the backyard, but he looked up when the door slid open.

"Oh, she called you," he said. "Figures."

I walked over and took a chair across from him. The porch was covered, but it was still warm. I now got a good look at him. His left eye was black and blue, and partially swollen shut. He had a cut above his right eyebrow, and the knuckles on his right hand looked scraped and bruised. He noticed me looking at his hand.

"Yeah, I got in one good shot," he said as he flexed his hand. "Unfortunately I hit the brick wall instead of the guy's face."

"Want to tell me about it?"

He slowly shook his head in disbelief as he stared past me. Michelle and Roger had a large backyard with flowerbeds, a freshly cut lawn, and plenty of trees for shade. Birds were chirping, and it would've seemed idyllic at another time. Dennis drew in a breath. "After you left, I went into Step Recovery for a minute, but then I came back outside for some air."

"Just air?" I asked pointedly.

He met my gaze. "I needed some air so I took a walk around the block. That's all. It was dark, and I passed an alley, and that's when someone jumped me. He yanked me into the alley, and I fell down. He kicked me in the side a couple of times and told me to back off. I managed to get to my feet, and that's when I took a swing at him but missed and hit the building."

"What else did he say?"

"He said stop digging up the past."

I sat back and contemplated him. "Meaning the blackmail, or something else?"

He blushed. "What else would it be?"

I casually picked at a thread on the armrest. "Whatever you and Singletary are covering up."

"This has nothing to do with whatever you think you overheard," He didn't sound so sure.

I had to laugh. "Why don't you tell me what you two are up to, and I can make that determination."

He shifted in the chair and grimaced. "Oh, man, my side hurts." He got a little more comfortable, then stared at me.

"I'm going to find whatever you're hiding."

"All I asked you to do was figure out who blackmailed me. That's it."

I nodded slowly. "And I told you I needed you to be truthful with me."

We weren't getting anywhere with this, so I returned to his assault.

"What did your attacker sound like? You're sure it was a man?"

"Yes. He had a low voice, and he was tall and thin. He wore a hoodie, a mask, and gloves, so I can't tell you what he looked like. When I tried to hit him, he belted me in the face, and I fell down again. Then he ran off." He gingerly touched near his eye.

"Could it have been the waiter from Billy's Restaurant?"

"I don't think so."

"You weren't robbed?"

He shook his head. "No, he beat me up. That's it. I got up, brushed myself off, and went back to Step. Michelle thinks I should have gone to the ER, but I've been beat up worse than this." He looked down at himself ruefully. "Nothing's broken; I can tell. I'll get over this."

We sat in silence for a moment, just the birds chirping. Someone started up a lawnmower down the street. Again, seemingly peaceful, but I couldn't dismiss the current of hostility between Dennis and me. I was tempted to quit the job right then. I wasn't getting anywhere, and he was lying to me about something. But I was also curious. I wanted to know what he was hiding, and as I told him, I was going to find that out.

"Taylor Walsh, the waiter from Billy's, saw the person who took the blackmail money, but he didn't have a good description, just a man in a hoodie and sunglasses."

He looked surprised. "You think maybe the same guy who attacked me last night?"

I shrugged. "That's what we need to find out. Was your attacker young, old?"

"I don't know. Maybe not that old, but how could I know? It was dark, and we were in an alley."

"It's not much to go on."

"Yeah. I wouldn't know how to track him down."

I mulled over what he'd told me. "There's more to this whole thing than you're telling me."

"Just find whoever blackmailed me." Another stretch of silence ensued. "You can call me with whatever you find," he finally said.

I nodded, got up, and walked back inside. Michelle and Roger were sipping coffee and peering out the sliding doors. Neither made any attempt to disguise that they'd been watching Dennis and me.

"So?" Michelle looked over her cup at me.

"Dennis has no idea who attacked him."

"Do you believe him?" Roger asked. Michelle glared at him.

I thought for a moment, then made eye contact with Michelle. "Do you think Dennis is hiding something?"

"Of course not," she quickly said. I glanced at Roger, and his look told me he didn't believe that.

"Whose idea was it to fire Dennis?" I asked.

"My father's." She avoided eye contact with Roger and me. I nodded slowly. "I want Dennis to get his life together," she tacked on.

I couldn't help with that, but I was going to find out what Dennis wasn't telling me.

"I'll keep you posted," I said.

I thanked them for their time and left.

CHAPTER SIXTEEN

I went out to my car, but I didn't leave. The dynamics between Michelle, Dennis, and Roger were curious to say the least. As I stared at the Farley house, I mulled over the case and came to a conclusion. I wanted to talk to Roger again without Dennis or Michelle being around. And it would be better that Michelle not know I was talking to her husband, either. That left me with a dilemma. I couldn't very well go back to Mowery Transportation, where they both worked, because she might see me with Roger. Given that, I made an impulsive decision and drove down the street, but I parked around the corner and watched the Farley house. It was a little after ten, but dark clouds were forming in the western sky. At this time of the year, Denver typically gets afternoon thunderstorms, but today rain was predicted on and off throughout the day. I glanced outside and wondered how long I would have before the clouds opened up. I also wondered how long it would be before I saw action at the Farley house. I listened to the Smiths and waited. Half an hour later, Roger emerged from the house and got into his truck. He backed out of the driveway and took off in the other direction. I worried that Michelle might come out of the house, and I didn't want her or Dennis to see me pass by. The truck reached the corner and turned right. I quickly started the 4-Runner, flipped a U-turn, and drove to the next block. At the end of the street, I saw the truck go by. I raced down the street, turned right, and saw Roger's truck up ahead. He drove to Alameda and headed south, and I swore quietly, worried that he was going directly back to Mowery Transportation. If that was the case, I probably wouldn't have much time to talk to him before Michelle showed up. But I caught a break when the truck turned into a Starbucks. Roger parked and strolled inside. I pulled in, parked, and followed him in. He was perusing the menu above the counter, and I stepped up behind him. He didn't notice me.

"Can I buy you a cup of coffee?" I asked.

He turned part way around, saw me, and his jaw dropped. "What do you want?"

"To ask you a few questions," I said. "Do you have a minute? My offer of coffee still stands."

He stepped aside. "Sure. I'll have a venti latte."

He stayed quiet, and when I reached the counter, I ordered a macchiato for myself and a latte for him. We moved aside to wait while our drinks were being prepared. He eyed me cautiously.

"What do you want to know?"

I didn't mince words. "You're not very fond of your in-laws."

He laughed wryly. "Oh, you caught that. Yeah, I guess I'm not. Especially Dennis."

"What do you know about the blackmailing?"

He shrugged. "Just what Michelle told me. I haven't talked to Dennis about it, because quite frankly, I don't know if he'd tell me the truth."

"You think he's lied about other things?"

He pondered that. "Probably. But don't ask for details. I don't want to get myself into trouble."

His firm gaze told me to move on, so I did. "Have you ever gotten along with Dennis?"

"Not really. He didn't like Michelle and I dating, and he wasn't happy when we got married. And the family seemed to think I should just join the business and work for them. I have my own ideas, business things that I could be doing. I don't have to rely on them all the time, you know."

"I get that. How much interaction did you have with Dennis around the office?"

"I'd see him around. He mostly stayed in his office."

"Did he go to the warehouses?"

He shook his head. "Why would he need to?"

I shrugged. "Just asking." Nothing from him. "Did you ever see him drunk at the office? Not handling himself professionally?"

He laughed derisively. "By the end, everybody did. He wasn't controlling himself very well, but I never had any reason to think he was skimming."

I looked pointedly at him. "You had no idea what Dennis was doing?"

The barista called out our names, and Roger took his drink. Then he stared back at me. "No, I didn't. And I need to get back to the office before Michelle wonders where I am." He held up the cup. "Thanks for the coffee."

With that, he walked purposefully out the door. I took my drink and walked after him. Not the friendliest guy, and one with a huge chip on his shoulder. He certainly didn't like his in-laws, or his work situation. He drove past me without a glance. I walked to my car and got in just as raindrops started falling. Something else had been on my mind since I'd talked to Dennis this morning. What if Taylor Walsh had come after him? If Walsh had been more involved in the blackmail scheme than he'd told Ace and Deuce, it was a possibility, although I couldn't figure out how Walsh would've tracked down Dennis. It was worth asking him, though.

The rain hit the car harder as I drove to Blazing Bistro, where Ace and Deuce had said Walsh now worked. I dashed through the rain into the restaurant. It was eleven o'clock, and a few people were seated at tables. I asked the hostess if Walsh was working today, and she said he was. Lucky for me. She sat me at a booth in his section, and a moment later, he approached with a menu.

"Can I get you something to drink?"

I ordered a Coke, then quickly perused the menu. "I'll have your

BLT," I said. It was not something I usually made at home, and it sounded good. "You're Taylor Walsh, correct?"

He nodded, curiosity in his eyes. "Yes. Do I know you?"

I decided to try to shake him up a little, get him off-balance. "What do you know about Dennis Mowery?"

He looked at me, puzzled. I couldn't tell if he was scared or not. "Who's that?"

"You were involved in blackmailing him, passing an envelope from him to someone else when you worked at Billy's."

He stared at me for a second, then backpedaled. "I'll have your order soon."

He spun on his heel and walked away. He poked his head in the kitchen, then paused at a soda station to get my Coke. He returned to the table, looking everywhere but at me.

"Taylor," I said in a low voice as I flashed my private investigator's license. Before I could say anything else, he held up a hand.

"Somebody already talked to me about this." His voice was low, pinched with fear. "I don't know anything, okay? I was looking to make a few bucks, that's all."

"Where were you last night about nine?"

His jaw tightened. "I was out with friends. Why?"

"My client, the man who'd been blackmailed, was beat up about that time. Whoever assaulted him told him to stop digging up the past." I took my straw and pointed at Walsh. "What if you were involved in the blackmail scheme, or you know who it was. Maybe you – or he – beat up my client."

Taylor glanced over his shoulder, then looked at me and shook his head vehemently. "I don't know anything about that, okay? Someone got my number, and I got a text asking if I would help with something." He turned red. "It went on from there, and then they gave me instructions about what to do. I don't know anything about who it was. You gotta believe me."

"You deal drugs, too?"

He shook his head, but I knew I was right. If he made extra money from that, he'd be willing to do something else – like pass on an envelope without asking questions – as well.

"Who were you with last night?" I asked.

"Two buddies of mine. We went skiing yesterday, and then to a bar. Look, I'll give you their names, okay?"

"They could lie for you," I pointed out.

He shook his head. "They won't." He perched on the edge of the seat opposite me, then pulled out his phone and consulted it. Then he tore a piece of paper from a notepad and wrote down two names and numbers. "You can call them right now."

I took the paper from him, looked at it, then looked up. "I will." I smiled broadly.

"I'm telling the truth," he whispered. "You gotta leave me alone, okay?" He glanced over his shoulder again, saw the hostess staring at him, and muttered, "I have to get back to work."

He got up and moved to another table, and I immediately called both his friends, Bryce Lindholm and Tony Alvarez. Walsh was watching out of the corner of his eye. Neither friend answered, and I didn't leave messages. I sipped my Coke and waited for my lunch, and when Walsh came back, he set my sandwich down and asked innocently, "Did you get hold of them?"

I shook my head. "No answer from either."

"I was with them."

"As I said before, they could lie for you."

He went pale, but he shrugged. "They won't." Then he mustered up some courage. "Leave me alone."

With that, he walked off. As I ate my lunch, I looked up Kim Mowery's number and called her. I left a message for her to call me back, and as I watched it rain, I finished my BLT. Walsh returned with a check, and I paid it. He didn't say another word. I sat for a minute, wishing the rain would stop. I finally ran through the downpour and was soaked by the time I got in the car. My phone rang: it was Kim returning my call.

"You're still looking into whatever this was with Dennis, huh?" she asked. I could hear the amusement in her tone.

"I've talked to a lot of people, and I've come up with more questions than answers."

She laughed. "When you're dealing with Dennis, that's not a surprise."

I ignored that. "When you and Dennis were still together, did he ever mention Warren Singletary?"

"Hmm. Not that I recall."

Something occurred to me that I'd not asked anyone. "How was it that Dennis hurt his knee? When he first had surgery and got the pain pills?"

"He slid on icy stairs on our front porch. It sure screwed up his knee."

"Could he have been keeping something else from you, besides stealing from the company? Was there some other kind of trouble that no one's told me about?"

"It could be," she said. Her laugh was short, almost a bark. "Who knows what all that man was hiding. At the end, I swear everything out of his mouth was a lie." Her bitterness toward her ex-husband wasn't helping me find answers.

"Would Michelle protect Dennis if he got into some other kind of trouble?"

"Of course. She dotes on him." She let out a heavy sigh. "I know you're trying to figure out what's going on, but I've been trying to move past my relationship with Dennis. And I really can't help you any more. I'm sorry."

"Okay, I understand."

I thanked her for her time and ended the call. I stared out the windshield. The rain wasn't letting up just yet.

CHAPTER SEVENTEEN

I called Clyde Hessler again, and he still didn't answer. I again asked him to call me, then ended the call and swore softly to myself. I decided to see if he had finally shown up at Mowery Transportation. The rain finally seemed to be letting up as I drove to Interstate 70. On the way, I mulled over the investigation. Sometimes a case just wouldn't break. I had a lot of information, but nothing fit together. That meant I needed to continue asking questions, hoping that something would finally make sense. However, my mind felt as dreary as the day. Even though I tried not to think about it, I was worrying about Willie. At a stoplight, I texted her and told her that I loved her. I knew I probably wouldn't get a reply back right away, but I wanted her to know.

The rain had eased to a light sprinkle by the time I arrived at Mowery, but dark clouds still hung heavy in the sky, threatening more. I parked in front of the office and went inside. Christie gave me a look as if she wanted to escape. Then she forced a smile.

"What can I do for you?" she asked. "Michelle isn't here right now."

I nodded. "Yes, but has Clyde Hessler come in?"

She shook her head. "No, I found out he's sick. He won't be in today."

She was rescued when Isaac came in. He openly sneered at me as he set some paperwork down on the desk in front of Christie.

"Could you get that mailed out today?" The tone was more an order than a request.

She nodded and glanced away. He didn't catch her wrinkling her nose in distaste, but I did. The tension between them was palpable. Isaac stared at me.

"You're back?" he stated the obvious.

I nodded. "Since I've caught you, maybe you can help me out."

He jerked a thumb for me to follow him. We walked outside just as a clap of thunder boomed. He started across the parking lot.

"Would it be possible for me to talk to any of the truck drivers?" I asked.

He called out to be heard over the sounds of trucks in the lot and on the street. "I know Michelle wants me to cooperate, but my drivers are busy. Hell, most of them aren't even here right now. It's a trucking company, you know? They're on the road. They have nothing to do with our financial operations. And they don't have access to the office after hours." He pointed at a rig. "You want another ride?"

"No, thanks." I dodged a puddle of water and caught up with him. "None of them would have any opportunity to go into the office? They wouldn't have known what Dennis was up to?"

He didn't answer as we walked into one of the warehouses. Then he whirled around and put his hands on his hips. "To answer your question, no. They're out on the road, and when they're here, they don't want to be *here*." He pointed at the ground. "They want to be home, with their families, their friends. And there would be very little reason for them to go into the office, so they wouldn't overhear anything."

I pointed back to the main office. "It doesn't seem like Christie likes you."

"You are blunt, aren't you?"

I smiled. "When I have to be. Right now I need to get some answers, so I don't have time for subtleties."

He laughed. "What Christie thinks of me is no business of yours."

I waited for some loud clanking to stop. "I'm trying to find a blackmailer. It could be practically anybody at the company."

"Even me?" The sarcasm was clear.

"Yeah, it could be you. I don't understand what motive you would have, but yes."

"You're right, I don't have a motive. If I'd caught Dennis stealing from the company, I would've confronted him."

I wondered what else he would've done to Dennis. "That makes sense to me. Let's go back to that tension between you and Christie."

He waved a hand. "It's nothing."

"That's not what I observed."

He muttered under his breath. "I don't know what her deal is. One night a while back, I was working late and I had to go into the office. She was down the hall, and she came back to the front, looking all nervous. I asked her what she was doing there so late, and she said she was finishing up some paperwork."

"You believed her?"

He paused. "I never really thought about it."

"And yet you just told me she wouldn't have been involved in any blackmailing."

"I guess I hadn't thought about that." Now he did appear to give that some consideration. "Geez, I don't know. She's been with the company a long time. I wouldn't think she'd do something like that."

"You haven't talked to Michelle about this?"

He shook his head. "It never occurred to me." But he was thinking about it now. He switched topics. "I heard Dennis got beat up last night."

"Yes, but he doesn't know who it was."

"Any number of people, I'm sure. I'll bet you found out that Dennis has pissed off a lot of people."

I eyed him. "Yes, and I've heard from more than one person that you and Dennis don't like each other."

He picked up a hammer from a workbench. "Yeah, whatever."

I watched him carefully. "You mentioned overhearing an argument between Warren Singletary and Dennis? Do you remember anything more about that?"

"No," he snapped. Too quick ... too guilty.

"There's more to your conversation with them than you're telling me."

He twirled the hammer in his hand.

"What's going on?" I was cautious with my tone.

He hesitated, then swore. "This sucks." He pointed with the hammer, and I edged back. I doubted he'd hit me right there, but part of me wasn't so sure. "I know that whatever I tell you, you're going to tell Michelle."

"Why are you worried about that?" I looked around and saw a man walk into the warehouse, and I suppressed a sigh of relief.

Isaac saw him and nodded. "Oh hell," he finally said to me. "I told you I saw Dennis and Warren talking, that they were arguing about something."

"Yes." I kept it short so he'd keep talking.

"I don't know what that was all about, something about it being an accident, and Dennis said no one would find out. But I was pissed at Dennis because he shouldn't have been here."

That puzzled me. "Here in the warehouse?"

He jabbed the hammer toward the front gate. "No. He shouldn't have been on the property at all. He'd already been fired, and he shouldn't have been here talking to anybody. I was furious at him for that, and I went after him. I shoved him back and told him to get the hell out of here, that he'd messed up his life, and that he wasn't welcome anymore. I called him a drunk, probably called him some other names, too. I don't remember what all I said." For once, his face softened. "I know that hurt him. I've never seen that kind of look on his face. He told me he was sorry, and then he left." His shoulders sagged a bit. "What I said crushed him, and I sometimes wonder if I made things worse for him, that he suddenly knew he'd disappointed his family so much. Michelle wondered the other day about how he must feel about what he did, his guilt and shame. Did that make it even harder for him to stop drinking? I wonder if I added to it." He suddenly cleared his throat and the swagger came back. "But you know what? That's not my problem."

I thought for a second. "What did Singletary do after you told Dennis to leave?"

"I told Warren to get back to work, and I watched until Dennis was off the property. I don't know where he went."

"Okay, I –" I stopped. "Wait a minute. When we talked before, I thought you meant the argument happened while Dennis was still working here."

He shook his head. "No, that argument happened after he was supposed to be gone."

"What do you think he and Singletary meant about an accident?"

He shrugged. "If Warren had been in an accident, it could've affected his CDL license. I checked into that, but didn't see a report of anything."

"Was Dennis ever in an accident?"

"Not that I know of. At that point, though, I didn't have a lot of contact with him. I hadn't seen him for weeks, didn't know where he was staying or what he was doing."

"Would Michelle know?"

He shook his head. "No, none of us had contact with him." A burly man in a black T-shirt and jeans waved at Isaac. He nodded, then looked at me. "I need to go."

Without another word, he turned on his heel and walked over to the other man. The two men conversed, but Isaac was watching me, making sure that I didn't venture farther into the warehouse. As long as he was holding that hammer, I wasn't going to. I smiled at him, left and walked across the parking lot. As I neared the office, a dark SUV pulled up next to my 4-Runner and Ben Mowery got out.

"Hello," I said politely.

He nodded at me and hurried into the building. He obviously didn't want to talk to me again. However, I wanted to talk to Christie again, so I followed him inside. He hurried down a hall and out of sight. Christie wasn't around. I waited a minute, then went back outside to call Michelle Farley.

"Hey, Reed," she said. She sounded flustered.

"How's Dennis?"

"He'll live. He wanted to go back to Step Recovery, so I dropped him off. I'm on my way to the office now."

"Hey, I was wondering, before he was fired, was he in some kind of accident?"

"Not that I know of."

"Have you heard anything from Clyde Hessler?"

"No. Why?"

"He didn't come into work today."

She didn't seem bothered by that. "He wouldn't have blackmailed Dennis."

"What about Christie Costa? I heard she's sometimes around after hours. Maybe poking around where she shouldn't be?"

"Where'd you hear that? Never mind, I'm sure you won't tell me. I don't know about her working late, though. She's hourly, so she'd have to put in for overtime. I'll find out, though."

"Does she ever help with the bookkeeping?" I asked casually.

"No." She blew out a breath. "And she wouldn't have blackmailed Dennis, either."

"Someone did."

She didn't reply for a moment, then said in a small voice, "I know."

CHAPTER EIGHTEEN

I sat for a minute in my car and stared into space. I'd accepted an investigation with myriad challenges, and there were a number of people who could've blackmailed Dennis. Try as I might, though, I was not seeing anything that pointed to a clear suspect. I needed to talk to Warren Singletary again, and I still hadn't been able to speak to Clyde Hessler. And I wondered if Taylor Walsh had been a mere go-between for Dennis's blackmailer, or if he knew more than he was saying. I needed to check his alibi, too. I tried his buddies, Bryce Lindholm and Tony Alvarez, again but neither one picked up. Again. Not surprising. I rubbed a hand over my face. One more thing to deal with. Unless ...

"O Great Detective, sorry I haven't returned your call. I got busy," Cal said when he answered my call. "I've been doing research on Grant Mowery, and Isaac and Michelle, like you asked. Nothing unusual so far. And nothing unusual about Dennis, either."

"Great," I said, disappointed.

"You wanted a flashing sign to point to someone's guilt?"

"Yeah, kind of."

He laughed. "I'll keep looking."

"Check Roger Farley, too. Michelle's husband. See what you can find there."

"Will do."

"One more thing," I went on. "Check into Christie Costa." I spelled the name. "She's the front-office person."

"She's ringing your suspicion meter?"

"Yes."

"I'll add her to the list."

"Thanks." Then I explained about Bryce Lindholm and Tony Alvarez. "I have phone numbers for them. Can you find their addresses?" I spelled the names.

"Yep, hang on." He hummed as he typed for a moment, then paused. "Got them. I'll text them to you."

"Way faster than me," I laughed. "Thanks."

I ended the call and tried Ace.

"Hey, Reed," he said. "You need any more help?"

"I do, if you have time."

"Sure!" He sounded so excited to help. "I'm at work now, but I get off at four and so does Deuce. Will that work?"

"Yes. I need you to talk to two of Taylor Walsh's friends." I explained how I was trying to verify Walsh's whereabouts the previous evening. "See what Lindholm and Alvarez tell you, and if you get any sense that either one is lying."

"Yeah, we can do that."

"I'm texting you their phone numbers and addresses. It should be pretty easy. Just report back what they say."

"You got it," he said. "When I get off work, I'll get Deuce and we'll see if we can track them down. We got this, Reed."

"I know you do."

I thanked him and smiled. I was curious how the Goofballs would handle this new assignment. I was sure that by now Walsh would have warned his two friends I'd be contacting them, but if Ace and Deuce showed up, what would Lindholm and Alvarez say to them? My gut said Walsh was telling the truth, and he hadn't assaulted Dennis, but it was a thread I still needed to check.

Getting help from the Goofballs freed me up for something else, namely tracking down Clyde Hessler. At this point, I felt as if he was dodging me, and I didn't like that. It didn't matter what Michelle or anyone else thought, I needed to talk to him. I pulled out my phone, got on a people-search site, and found where he lived. It was time for a chat with him, and then with Warren Singletary. But the best laid plans often get derailed. My phone rang, a number I vaguely recognized.

"Reed Ferguson," I said officiously.

"This is John Talbot, returning your call."

"Dennis's friend," I said.

"He and I knew each other a while back. Your message said you needed to talk to me. I'm headed out to lunch. Could you meet me?"

"That'd be great," I said, even though I'd already eaten lunch when I'd talked to Taylor Walsh.

"I'm downtown. There's a Hopdoddy's Burger Bar near Seventeenth and Wynkoop. I'm headed there now."

"I'm not too far away, so I'll see you soon."

"I'm in tan slacks and a blue shirt. I'll sit outside."

"Great."

I ended the call and made a beeline toward downtown. And then my phone rang again.

"Reed, dear. How are you?" a high-pitched feminine voice said.

"Hello, Mom. I'm okay, I'm on a new case."

"Nothing dangerous, I hope?"

I've been a PI for years, but no matter how much I reassure my mother that it's rarely dangerous, she can't seem to believe me. Admittedly, it doesn't help that I have indeed run into trouble now and again, but on most cases, I don't receive a scratch. She also used to worry that I was doing drugs, no matter how much I protested that I didn't, and despite the fact that she had absolutely no reason to think so. She's finally let that go, and she doesn't ask about it anymore. I guess that's progress.

"You don't sound so good," she said. "Is everything all right?"

My mind was already on other things, and then I thought of Willie's upcoming exam. I wasn't hiding things well. I bit my lip, though, as much as I wanted to say something. "No, it's okay."

"How's Willie?"

It was like getting hit in the gut. "She's okay," I said. "Just the usual stuff."

I hated to keep my mother in the dark, but Willie was right. If we said anything to my mother now, she would do nothing but worry, and she'd likely call and bug Willie and me to death.

"Well," she stretched out the word. "If you say so."

"How are *you* doing, Mom?" I asked to change the subject.

"I'm doing fine, dear, and so is your father. We went golfing this morning, and now we're relaxing. Well, he fell asleep in a chair on the deck."

My parents lived in Denver when I was growing up, but they'd retired to Florida a few years ago. They both love to golf, love socializing with their friends, and my mother loves to tell me everything that's going on, sometimes in excruciating detail. She did so now, telling me about a lovely dinner – her words – they had with some friends of theirs the previous evening. I listened as I drove, and then suddenly I realized she was saying, "Are you sure you're okay?"

"Yes, I am. I've got some case stuff on my mind, and I'm meeting somebody soon for lunch."

"Oh, I'm sorry, I can let you go. Why don't you talk to Willie about visiting soon, okay?"

I nodded. "Yes, we'd love to see you and Dad. I love you, Mom."

"I love you too, dear. So does your father."

"Tell him hello."

"I will when he wakes up."

I ended the call and pushed down a wave of anxiety that threatened to overwhelm me. Willie would be okay. She just had to be. I stared at the cars in front of me and weaved my way into downtown. When I got to Hopdoddy's Burger Bar, John Talbot was sitting at a table outside. He waved me over and I sat down. An umbrella shielded us from a stray raindrop or two.

"I hope you don't mind eating outside?" He glanced at the clouds. "I think we're safe for the moment, although I think the rain is supposed to pick up later."

I nodded. "This is fine. It's a nice break from the heat."

"I don't have very long, I'm sorry. I've already ordered."

I picked up a menu and glanced at it. "No problem. I've already eaten so I'll get a drink."

"I'm sorry. I didn't know."

"It's okay. I appreciate your taking the time to meet with me."

He smiled as a waiter approached. I ordered a Coke, then handed the menu to the waiter. When he left, John looked at me.

"I haven't heard the name Dennis Mowery in quite some time. How is he?"

"Well, he's been having some serious issues. But he's trying to get back on his feet. He's clean and sober now, living at a halfway house. You haven't talked to him?"

He shook his head. "No. The last time I talked to Dennis was, gosh, over a year ago or more."

"How did he seem to you?"

"To be honest, he didn't look particularly well." He frowned. "So you know about his drug and alcohol issues." I nodded, and he went on. "He used to be fun to hang around, but he started getting out of control. He'd drink too much, was probably popping pills. He'd slur his words, and it was hard to follow him. It wasn't fun then. I begged him to get some help, but he wouldn't do it, said he didn't have a problem. But it was getting worse and worse." He shrugged. "There's only so much you can do."

"Was anything going on that contributed to his behavior?" I kept my question vague to see what he knew or would share.

Before he answered, the waiter returned with a hamburger and fries for him, and my Coke. John took a bite of his burger, then said, "From what I could gather, Dennis had a lot going on. Things weren't good with his wife, Kim, and it wasn't good at work, either." He squirted ketchup on his plate, dipped a couple of fries into it, and popped them into his mouth. "Oh, those are good. Anyway, Dennis told me a couple of times that Michelle and his dad weren't happy with him, and they were getting on his case. I'd tell him he needed to clean up his act, but he'd brush that off. Then one night he called me, drunk, maybe high, and certainly upset. He was still at work, even though it was after hours. He ..." He hesitated and stalled by taking another bite of his burger.

"What?" I tried to keep it casual and sipped my Coke, but I was worried he'd hold back on whatever was bothering him.

He stopped eating for a moment and leaned in. "He admitted he was stealing from the company. I knew then he was in real trouble."

I held up a hand. "Wait. You knew about that?"

He picked at his fries. "I'll never forget it. He was drunker than a skunk. He told me he'd made a terrible mistake, that he was spending too much money, and then he finally said he was skimming from his family's company. I couldn't believe he told me that. It wasn't like Dennis at all, not the Dennis I knew, anyway. I asked him why, and he hesitated, then said he needed the money to pay for the pills, that it was expensive. At that point, I knew that he must've been using a lot. I told him it was time to get some help, and he just laughed. Then he suddenly got quiet and said he thought someone might be outside his office. I asked who, but he didn't know. He started whispering and said he needed to go. He wasn't making a lot of sense, and he ended the call shortly after that." He frowned. "I didn't talk to him very many times after that, and I urged him to talk to his family about what he'd been doing. He got really angry at me for that and told me I'd better not tell anyone. It seemed like he was spiraling downward, wouldn't return my calls. I talked to him one final time and told him that he needed to get some help, but he wouldn't listen. Then I lost touch with him." He dipped another fry in ketchup but didn't eat it. "I told Dennis I wouldn't tell anyone what he was up to, but I guess I just blew that, didn't I?"

I didn't answer that. "Do you remember when that phone call was?"

"It was the fall, Monday night." He smiled. "I don't remember the exact date, but Monday Night Football was on, the Broncos and the Bears. Dennis didn't like football, but he knew I did, and he was asking why I was wasn't watching the game. He was too out of it to realize he'd called me." He sighed. "He lost his job after that. I can't say I blame them for firing him."

"Did you tell anyone about the skimming?"

"No." He set the napkin down and took a drink. "Why all the questions now?"

I watched him closely. "You don't know anything else?"

His brow furrowed. "No. What's going on?"

"Someone found out Dennis was stealing from the company, and they blackmailed him, said they would tell unless he paid them off. That's part of why he needed money."

He swore softly. "So he skimmed even more money."

"You didn't know?"

"He never mentioned it." He sighed. "Wow. He was in real trouble, wasn't he?" Then something occurred to him. "You think I would do that to him?"

I stared at him. "It's a thought. I've been hired to find the blackmailer."

He wasn't defensive at all. "Dennis was my friend, and I'd never do something like that to him. You check into me all you want, and you'll find I'm telling the truth."

"You didn't tell anyone what Dennis was doing?"

"Not a soul, til now."

"Why not?"

"I didn't think it was my place, and I didn't want him to get into any trouble with the law. But I begged him to try to make it right, try to work it out with his family. I don't know if that was the right thing to do or not."

"Did Dennis ever mention some kind of accident that he was involved in?"

"Not that I recall." He finished the fries and pushed his plate back, and checked the time on his phone. "I hate to rush, but I do need to get back to work." He started to pull out his wallet, but I waved him off.

"I've got this."

"Thanks," he said. "I've got your number, in case I think of anything else."

I nodded and watched him walk away from the restaurant. He merged into the crowd, and I sipped my Coke and thought through what he'd told me. Whether he realized it or not, he was now a suspect. He could've blackmailed Dennis. I wasn't sure I bought that. It'd be a heartless thing to do to your friend. However, Talbot could've told someone else, who then blackmailed Dennis. And Talbot had seemed genuine when he said he hadn't told a soul. Regardless, I was still going to look into him. I pulled out my phone and googled the

Broncos-Bears game and found the exact date it had been played. If my memory was correct, Dennis had said that he'd received the first blackmail note shortly after that game, shortly after he'd drunkenly admitted to John that he'd been stealing from the company.

Another thing went through my mind: Someone might've overheard Dennis talking on the phone to John. And if so, that person, whoever it was, might have decided to cash in on the situation through a little blackmail.

CHAPTER NINETEEN

I paid the check and left the hamburger joint. As I walked to my car, my mind raced. I finally had some useful information. I just wasn't sure how it pointed to a blackmailer. And I hadn't talked to Clyde Hessler yet. I wanted to follow up on John Talbot, but it was high time I tracked down Hessler. A few pesky raindrops fell as I got into my car and drove to his place, a small ranch-style house in Lakewood, off Wadsworth and Alameda.

The sky was gray, and dark clouds lurked to the east as I parked and got out. I walked past a black truck parked in the Hessler driveway. Small flower beds ran the length of a covered front porch, and the yard was green and lush. I rang the bell and waited, then rang again. Christie Costa had said that Hessler was sick, so why wasn't he answering? Too sick to come to the door? I was tempted to peer into a front window, but the curtains were closed. I could walk around the house and peek in other windows, but if Hessler was home and under the weather, I would have a lot of explaining to do. I decided not to and walked back to my car. A high school with a large parking lot sat empty across the street. Fall classes hadn't started yet. I waited a moment, then drove around the block and parked at the far end of the school parking lot. Then I watched Hessler's house. I listened to a few songs. I carry granola bars in the car, and I ate one. Willie texted and said she was doing okay, that she loved me. It started to rain lightly. A car drove past, but the Hessler house stayed quiet. I called him again and still got no answer. Then I noticed the curtains in the Hessler front room move. I sat up straight and watched. Sure enough, someone was peeking out, probably watching me. Good. Time for some action.

I started the 4-Runner, cut across the parking lot and exited near the Hessler house. I parked again and stalked up to the front door. I rang the bell, then knocked for good measure. The curtains remained closed. However, this time a man I thought to be about fifty opened the door. He was trim and muscular, about my height. A full head of dark hair was in disarray. He wore sweats, a wrinkled maroon-colored T-shirt, his feet bare.

"Yes?" He cleared his throat, then coughed.

"You're Clyde Hessler?" I asked. He nodded. "I'm Reed Ferguson. I tried to get hold of you at Mowery Transportation, and –"

"Didn't Christie tell you I sounded sicker than a dog?" he snapped.

I shook my head. "Just that you weren't feeling well."

He hacked, a bit exaggerated. He covered his mouth with his hand, then waved it around. I took a subtle step back. I didn't want to be quite so close to a petri dish.

"I feel like crap, okay? I've been home yesterday and today both."

"I'm sorry, but I do need to talk to you. It's important."

He stared at me with bleary eyes. "Yeah, Michelle told me about you. I figured you'd be stopping by." He squinted past me to the school parking lot, a not-so-subtle way of letting me know he'd seen me there. "Not today, though."

"I rang the bell before. No one answered."

"I was asleep, and my wife's at work."

"When did Michelle speak with you? I thought no one had talked to you recently."

He shook his head, then seemed to regret it as he grimaced. "Damn headache." He glared at me. "I really wanted to ignore the doorbell, but I saw you parked across the street. I figured you really needed to talk to me."

Busted, I thought. But at least my surveillance got him to open the door.

"Did Michelle fill you in on the situation at the office?" I asked.

Now he put a hand against the door jamb, transferring germs, I was sure. "Yeah, Michelle told me all about Dennis." His voice sounded like a dull saw blade cutting wood. "I couldn't believe it, but Dennis was quite a handful before he was let go."

I took another step back and leaned against the porch railing. "Did you have any idea what Dennis was doing?"

Another cough. "No, I didn't. He handled all the accounting."

"As office manager, you didn't look at the books at all?"

His attention strayed to the yard and the rain. "Well, sure, sometimes. I had to check things, run reports, help with submitting bids. Things like that. There was a lot going on from day to day."

I crossed my arms. "You never saw anything suspicious?"

He cleared his throat, then pulled a cough drop from his sweatpants and popped it into his mouth. "No, I didn't. I'll tell you what, now I'd like to go back through the books to see how he did it. Dennis is a smart guy, though. He would've been careful. He would've taken a little bit here and a little bit there so that it would be harder to notice." A menthol smell drifted to me, and I wrinkled my nose. "There's a lot of ways to skim off a company."

"Did you have petty cash?"

"Sure, but I wouldn't think enough to entice him." He seemed to reconsider that. "Now that I think about it, sometimes when I checked it, the numbers didn't add up. You think he stole that?"

I shrugged. "As you said, there are a lot of ways to skim money." I thought for a second. "You helped with bids and contracts?"

"I looked at a lot of that. But I didn't look closely enough, now did I?"

It was part accusatory, part guilt.

"What if you'd found out what Dennis was doing?" I asked.

Something flashed in his eyes. "I would've told Grant and Michelle. Why? You think I would've blackmailed Dennis?"

I stared at him. "As I've said numerous times to other people, somebody knew what Dennis was doing, and they didn't tell Grant or

Michelle. It sounds as if you had access to the same books and records that Dennis did."

He started to protest, coughed, then put a hand over his mouth again. "Sure, I had access to all of that, but so did a lot of other people." He huffed for a moment. "Michelle called me and said you'd be coming by. I had no idea about what." A faint smile crossed his face. "I've liked working with Michelle, and I give her credit now. She could've warned me about you, but she wanted you to get a genuine reaction from me." He put his hands on his hips. "Well, you're going to get a genuine reaction." He swore. "If you think I had anything to do with Dennis's blackmail, or that I knew what he was doing, you're wrong. And I challenge you to find anything different."

I nodded appreciatively at his candor. "And if I find that I'm wrong, you can get an apology from me."

"An apology isn't necessary. You find out what happened."

Was he protesting too much? My suspicion meter was dinging loudly in my head. I switched directions. "Have you seen Dennis recently?"

"He's at a halfway house, but I haven't seen him. I don't think anyone would want him around the office now, not with what's happened."

"How do you know where he's living?"

He was suddenly evasive. "I don't know. Someone must've mentioned it."

"I've asked this of everyone else, but when Dennis still worked at Mowery, did you notice anything strange with him, beyond that he was drunk or high?"

"Not really." He rubbed his chin, stalling. "You want to know what goes on in that company, talk to the family. Ben's been there after hours, and Michelle's husband, Roger's all over the place, floating between all the departments, keeping tabs on operations. Roger can't sit still, hasn't from the day I started there."

"How long have you been with the company?"

"I started a few years before Dennis quit. It's been a good job." He didn't sound that convincing.

I glanced to the driveway. "Nice truck."

"Yeah, I got it a little over a year ago. Always wanted one. It's fun to drive."

"I'll bet," I said. "I've heard other people describe Mowery Transportation as a family kind of place. Do you feel that way?"

He shrugged and coughed. "It's all right, I guess." He stopped, and I stared at him. He raised a hand. "There's always something between Isaac and Dennis. And Dennis and Roger. Huh. I guess that *is* kind of like family, fighting with each other." He laughed, then started hacking.

"Fighting about what?"

"Oh, geez, I don't know."

"Speaking of Roger, I got an ear full from him about how he'd dreamed of branching out and doing his own thing."

He shrugged carefully. "I don't know about that. He hasn't seemed too happy that his son is working at the company, though."

"Oh?"

He let out a little laugh that turned into another cough. "I don't know. Andy's nice, quiet. Smart. It seems to me like it could be a pretty good gig for a young kid. He's being shown the ropes, is getting training, and he can get an idea of what he wants to do, even if it's not at Mowery Transportation."

"Sounds pretty good to me, too."

He smiled. "Yeah, but maybe he doesn't like working with his family, just like Roger."

"Have you met the younger son, Jordan?"

"At some company picnics, that kind of thing. He's not like Andy. If either of them are going to give their parents trouble, it's Jordan. I hear things about him."

I ventured a guess. "You don't like him."

He eyed me. "I have to be careful what I say."

"I'll keep it between us." His mouth was a thin line, noncommittal. "What do you think about Grant and Ben? And Michelle?"

He narrowed his eyes. "You realize you're trying to get me to speak about my bosses?"

I nodded casually. "Yes, and whatever you say stays here. I'm also trying to find a blackmailer, who seemingly had to be somebody within that company."

He didn't say anything for a moment. "I like Grant and Michelle. They've treated me well."

A careful answer. "Ben?"

"I don't work with him."

I moved on. "Can you think of anybody else that might've had access to the books, might have known what Dennis was doing?"

"No." His cough drop clacked on his teeth.

I pressed him a bit about Christie and Isaac, and he didn't have much to say, other than that Isaac was brash, but that he didn't have a lot to do with him. Hessler started a hacking fit again, and this time I wasn't subtle when I took a step back.

"I don't mean to be rude," he said, "but if you want to ask more questions, it should be another time. I really don't feel well."

I nodded and resisted covering my face. "Thanks for talking to me now. Just one more thing," I said, sounding like Peter Falk's Columbo. "Where were you last night?"

He glared at me. "I was here. I'm sick, you know."

I smiled without humor. I didn't ask for more details, but I was going to check on his whereabouts. "If I have any other questions, I know where to find you."

His eyes narrowed. "That you do." He quickly shut the door.

I hurried in the rain to my car and hopped in. Through the drops on the windshield, I could see Hessler peeking out again through the front window curtains. I was tempted to wave at him. He'd explained a lot and had given me a lot to think about, but I wasn't sure I bought any of it. And he knew where Dennis Mowery was living. Had Hessler beaten him up? I considered that. Had Hessler been involved in blackmailing Dennis? I frowned. Hessler deserved more attention. And so did John Talbot. I had two guys now who both had dared me to look into their backgrounds. Cocky because they were innocent, or because that was a way to point me in another direction?

I was going to look into both, regardless.

CHAPTER TWENTY

As much as I wanted to follow up on Clyde Hessler's alibi, I still hadn't heard from Warren Singletary, the truck technician, so I called him again. I was sure he was screening his calls and avoiding me, but I needed to talk to him. Fifteen minutes later, I was standing on his front porch. I knocked and rang the bell, but he didn't answer. I chewed on that for a moment. When I'd stopped by before, in the middle of the day, he was there, working. So why wasn't he home now?

I went back to my car, pulled out my phone, and googled his name. I couldn't find a LinkedIn page with his work history, and I didn't find anything else, no social media pages, nothing but basic information on people-search sites. However, I'd have to pay to learn more from those sites. I pocketed my phone and stared at Singletary's house. Curtains covered the front window. I got out and tried the door again. Still no answer. I looked around. The neighborhood was quiet.

Should I?

I stepped off the porch and stole around the side of the house, but encountered a gate with a sign that read, "Beware of Dog." I peeked into the back yard. It was small, the porch cluttered with an old wooden picnic table, a barbecue grill, and some old tires and car parts. A rickety doghouse sat in the back corner. I couldn't tell if a dog was in it or not. The clouds were clearing, but with a wet lawn, and the possibility of running from an angry dog, I decided not to chance sneaking into the yard. I swore softly and hurried back to my car.

I texted Dennis and told him to call me as soon as he could, then quickly googled Clyde Hessler and found that his wife was named Glenda. After a bit of searching, I found a LinkedIn page that listed her work: Western Biochemical, off Sixth and Wadsworth, which was just a little north of where I was. Traffic wasn't too bad, and I arrived there in short order.

Western Biochemical was in a five-story red brick building surrounded by tall bushes and a few evergreen trees that yearned for water. As I walked inside, I had the feeling the building had been neglected. A large "For Lease" sign hung in a window next to the entrance. The atrium was drab with a stale odor. A fountain had no water running, and a couple of planters held a few wilting plants in them. I went to a directory next to the elevators, and the listings were sparse. Western Biochemical was on the third floor. The elevator groaned its way up, and I walked worn carpet to their office. A perky young receptionist smiled at me.

"May I help you?"

"I'd like to see Glenda Hessler."

I was prepared to flash my investigator's license, but all she did was keep the smile as she picked up a desk phone for a quick call. Then she hung up and pointed down the hall.

"She's the third office on the right."

That was easy, I thought. I thanked her and headed down the hall. I tapped on an open door with Glenda's name on it and looked inside. Glenda was about Clyde's age, with grayish-blond hair, bright blue eyes, and wire-rimmed glasses perched on a long nose. She wore a white blouse that drained the color from her face. She gestured for me to come in. She turned down the soft rock music playing on her computer and contemplated me.

"I thought my afternoon appointment was later."

I sank into a stuffed chair and looked at her. "Who's your appointment?"

She pushed up her glasses. "My guy with the chemical reports for the project in Durango. You?"

I shook my head. "Sorry, not me." Now I knew why it had been so easy for me to see her. "I'm here about a different matter."

"Oh?"

Now I did show my investigator's license. She leaned forward, and I got a whiff of perfume. I tried to keep it casual. "I'm in the middle of an investigation at Mowery Transportation, where your husband works."

A wrinkle formed between her eyes. "I hope nothing's wrong."

I shook my head. "Just some routine questions. I visited with your husband earlier."

She drew in a breath. "He's had a cold the last couple of days," she said, not sounding convinced. "It's strange, Clyde never gets sick, and suddenly he seems like he just can't quit coughing. I've avoided him because I don't want to get whatever he has." She was talking fast, nervous. "I hope someone at his work didn't complain? He's got a great record there. He's been a great employee, at least that's what I hear from Michelle and the others at company parties."

I smiled. "It's nothing like that. And yes, he was coughing some. He's been home for the last couple of days?"

She nodded. "Yes, except for last night, when he went out to get more medication. I had gone out with some friends." She blushed. "I didn't want to be around him and his germs, the coughing. When I came home, he said he'd gone to the grocery store. Then I felt guilty because I should've been the one doing that. I did get mad at him, told him that he should've called me and I could've picked up something, but you know men ..." She turned even redder as she realized she was talking to me. "Well, you guys don't always want to ask for help, and you can kind of be babies when you get sick."

"My wife says the same thing about me," I said. I didn't say anything about her not being able to confirm Clyde's alibi. "Your husband has been at Mowery Transportation for several years?"

"Yes. He was with a construction company, and he decided he wanted a change of pace. There was more opportunity at Mowery Transportation. It's been great, quite frankly. He's making more money, and it's allowed us to do a few more things, especially now that the kids are on their own. We've been able to do some traveling, and do some remodeling around the house."

"And buy a new truck?" I asked.

She smiled. "Oh, Clyde and that truck. He's so proud of it. It cost a lot of money, but he'd gotten a nice bonus at work so he said we should buy it. I'm not fond of it, but he loves it." She gave a small shrug.

"I can see that. It's a nice truck."

I chatted with her for a few more minutes about Mowery Transportation, and I kept it vague. She never did ask me what exactly I was investigating, and then her desk phone beeped. She picked it up, spoke for a second, and then cradled the receiver with a look at me.

"My afternoon appointment is here, so I'm going to have to cut this short." She almost seemed disappointed that we couldn't chat more.

I smiled. "Thank you, I appreciate your time."

"I'm not sure what this is about, but ..."

I stood up and left her office before she had a change of heart and asked me what was going on. Whether she realized it or not, she not only hadn't verified Clyde's alibi for last evening, but in my mind, she'd planted more suspicion on him. More scrutiny for him.

The sky began to clear as I headed home. Humphrey was delighted to see me – only because Willie wasn't there, I was sure – and I gave him a couple of treats while I got a glass of water. Then I hurried into my office and sat down at my desk. Humphrey came in and curled up on my lap while I worked.

I got on the computer and searched on Clyde Hessler. I found a bio for him on LinkedIn that listed his previous employment at Big Cat Construction, and before that he'd been with a small accounting firm. I poked around the internet some more but didn't find much else on him. He had a son and daughter, both in their twenties, but try as I might, I couldn't find anything else noteworthy.

After draining my water, I checked on John Talbot. I found that he worked at a law firm downtown, and that he was married with three children, two boys and a girl. I did find an Instagram page for him, mostly posts of him with his family traveling. After scrolling through a lot of posts, I noticed one with him and Dennis at a bar. They both looked good, Dennis certainly better than he did now. I finally sighed in frustration. With both Hessler and Talbot, I hadn't found anything suspicious from a financial standpoint, and nothing that would help me determine whether one or the other might be a blackmailer. And without being able to get more in-depth into their banking and financial situations, I probably wouldn't. It was time to call in the big gun.

"Cal," I said when he answered. "What're you doing?"

"I'm headed down to Sunshine Cupcakes," he said. A hum buzzed through the phone, and I supposed he was talking from his car phone. "I'm going to help her with some cleanup in the shop after she closes for the day."

Holly had certainly stolen Cal's heart. For him to want to help her clean up was a beautiful thing. A few years ago, he likely wouldn't have ventured out of his house.

"Do you have your laptop with you?"

"Of course," he said. "I need to monitor some work things. You know me, I work all the time."

That was true. His schedule was erratic, not much of a schedule at all, really. He often toiled in the middle of the night. But that worked in my favor now.

"Would it be all right if I met you there? I need your help with some in-depth research on a couple of suspects."

"Sure, I can do that. Oh, one thing I did find. It looks like Roger Farley had some money tied up with a company called Imperial Supply. It looked like a bad deal. They sell supplies to trucking companies."

"Hmm," I said. "He mentioned wanting to branch out, but he didn't tell me he'd actually done it. And neither did Michelle."

"I haven't had a chance to look at the company, but I didn't see anything fishy. Maybe Roger just didn't want her to know he'd screwed up."

"Yeah." Based on what Roger had told me, I could see that. I filed away the information. "I'll see you soon."

With that, he was gone. I put Humphrey on his kitty bed on the desk and gave him a kiss. He stretched, meowed, then curled up. Not a care in the world. I had a feeling it might be a long night, so I texted Willie that I would be late, then headed out the door.

CHAPTER TWENTY-ONE

When I walked into the Sunshine Cupcake Shop, Holly Durocher was behind the counter. She glanced at me and waved, then continued helping a customer.

"These are white cupcakes with raspberry filling," she was explaining, "and these are turtles, with caramel and chocolate drizzle, and pecans."

I stepped up. "They're all fantastic."

The customer smiled at me, then took two of each. Holly rang up the order and thanked the woman, and waved to her she walked out the door. Holly smiled at me.

"That was sweet of you."

"I wasn't lying." I moved up to the counter and my mouth watered as I perused the variety of cupcakes. "Oh, I haven't tried these pumpkin ones."

"It's a new recipe. I'm testing it now, and if it goes over well, we'll be selling them in the fall."

"I'll try one of them." I started to get out my wallet and she shook her head. "Oh, honey, for you it's free."

I took the cupcake from her. "You don't have to do that."

"You should charge him double, just because it's Reed," Cal said as he emerged from the back room.

He wore khakis and a polo shirt, a white apron tied around his waist. I cocked an eyebrow at him. There was a time when Cal couldn't care less about his appearance, but he looked sharp now. I told him so.

"Even with an apron," I tacked on.

He held up his hands. "Hey, I'm learning to bake, too."

I tried the pumpkin cupcake. "This is delicious!"

"Oh, good." Holly beamed.

She began wiping down the counter. "Shalise, my baker, couldn't make it in today. I have a few big orders for birthday parties, and I really needed the help." The smile she gave Cal was warm and full of – dare I say it – love. "Cal's so sweet to come down and help. And he picks up stuff really quickly."

For Cal to have to learn anything was a rare thing. Cal knew more about almost everything than most people, although at times he lacked any common sense.

"Yes, but you'll have to show me what to do." Cal pointed behind him. "I'm not quite sure how you fill these cupcakes." He held one up.

"Oh, let me show you." She looked at me. "Can you watch the front for a minute?"

"Sure," I said. "But I hope no one comes in."

"Holler if they do."

Holly and Cal disappeared into the back, and I sat down at a small round table near the counter and finished the cupcake. I might be able to track down murderers – and maybe even a blackmailer – but I didn't want to run the register. But – of course – someone came in. The woman approached the counter and perused the cupcake selection.

"How are these white raspberry cupcakes?" she asked.

"They're fantastic," I said. It wasn't a lie. I love the white raspberry cupcakes.

"Okay, I'll take two of those," the woman said, looking at me.

I popped up and poked my head into the kitchen. Holly was hunkered over the table, and she was completely engrossed in showing Cal how to fill a cupcake. She didn't even look up. And Cal looked perplexed in a way I'd never seen him to be. I hated to interrupt them. Maybe I could handle this myself.

I hurried around the counter, found a container, and put two cupcakes in it. I glanced toward the kitchen, hoping Holly would emerge and rescue me. That didn't happen, so I continued to help the customer. She ordered four more cupcakes, and then went to the register and handed me a credit card.

"Okay," I muttered. I'd seen people scan my card. How hard could it be? Hmm. Harder than I thought. I had to find the correct size cupcakes, then make sure I included tax. I finally updated the order, and the woman paid. After a bit of fumbling, I finally figured out the credit card device. Then she smiled, took her cupcakes, and headed out the door. I glanced at the register. A fifteen percent tip. Not bad.

I stayed behind the counter, and thankfully, for me at least, no one else came in. A few minutes later, Holly emerged from the kitchen, blowing her bangs out of her eyes and rubbing filling off her hands with a clean towel, then nodded over her shoulder.

"Cal says to go on back."

"Thanks," I said.

I headed through the door into a small kitchen. It smelled sweet, and rock music played softly. Cal was standing at a metal table, intently inserting the pastry tip of a piping bag to fill a cupcake with a chocolaty filling. There were dozens more cupcakes lined up in pans on the table, waiting to be filled.

"Have you found your second career?" I asked.

His brow furrowed as he concentrated. He squeezed the bag carefully, hesitated and stopped, then squeezed the bag again. "I hope I don't screw this up. Holly will kill me."

I glanced over my shoulder. "I don't think so."

He finished with the cupcake and held it up. "I think this one's okay." He put it on a tray and said, "What can I help you with?"

I sat down at a little table with two chairs in the corner. Cal already had his laptop set up. I leaned back in the chair. "I'm running all around with this investigation, and I'm not coming up with much." I filled him in on everything that I'd done and finished with my interview with Glenda Hessler. "I want to dig into Clyde Hessler and John

Talbot more. I'm not sure what I think of Talbot, but Hessler has really got me suspicious. I don't trust him at all."

He gestured with the piping bag. "I can help you, but I'll have to talk you through how the software works while I keep working on these."

It was my turn to hesitate. "My trying to use your security software should be as good as you helping Holly fill those cupcakes."

He tipped his head at me and picked up cupcake number two. "Haha, you're funny. You can handle it. You see the icon with the two green checkboxes on the desktop? Open that up."

I pulled the laptop to me and opened up the software. "Now what?"

"Type in my password." He gave it to me, then stopped to focus on filling the cupcake, then examined it with dissatisfaction. "See the menu on the right? Open that, and type in Hessler's name."

I did as instructed, and he walked me through the next several steps. I looked up at him. "What's next?"

He set down a cupcake, came over and pointed out a few more things, and we ran through a couple more programs.

"I need to see Hessler's finances for a few years."

"Sure. Do this."

More instructions to me, more pointing at his laptop with the piping bag as he filled another cupcake. He still had the intense look on his face as he slowly squeezed more chocolaty filling into the cupcake. I hoped Holly wasn't in a huge hurry for the cupcakes to be finished.

"One more completed," he muttered as he inspected the cupcake.

"Please tell me I can't run transactions through Hessler's bank," I said.

Cal shook his head. "Don't be ridiculous. That would be illegal as well as highly unethical. This is just a report."

"Good," I muttered as he walked back to the table.

He guided me through a few more incredibly painstaking maneuvers, and then I waited. He picked up the next cupcake, treating it as if it were a fragile egg. I watched him with amusement. After a minute, he had me open up a file. "What do you see?"

My eyes widened. "I can't believe it's pulled up all this financial information," I said just as Holly walked in.

She looked back and forth between Cal and me. "I'm not going to ask what the two of you are doing." She eyed me. "It's amazing what Cal can come up with, and it's scary, too. I'm glad he's on the good guys' side."

"You better believe it," Cal said. "I'm the one helping keep the hackers from you."

She kissed him on the cheek. "Yes, you are." She looked at the table. "How are these cupcakes coming along?" Her eyes widened when she saw only three cupcakes with filling in them.

"Not too bad," he said.

"Oh, yes." She glanced at me. The look said she was in trouble. Cal wasn't moving along nearly fast enough. "Um, Cal, let me help you."

"I'm doing fine," he said.

"Yes, we just ... need to get these finished." She smiled, and he nodded.

"Well, okay, if you insist ..." He seemed only slightly deflated to have Holly step in to help.

As Holly grabbed the pastry bag and began filling the cupcakes like the pro she was, Cal and I just sat back and watched in awe. Then I stared at the laptop. The software had gotten into the Hessler accounts, and I was able to look at his finances, specifically around the time that Dennis had been blackmailed. However, I couldn't find any large deposits into the accounts. I sat back and thought for a moment. I did find what appeared to be one large deposit for ten grand from Mowery Transportation, a much higher amount than his normal paychecks. I mulled on that, then picked up my phone and called Mowery Transportation and asked for Michelle.

"This is Michelle," she said, her voice hurried.

"Hey, it's Reed."

"Oh, do you have an update for me?"

"I'm still looking into a lot of things."

"I hope you find something. I'm worried about Dennis. He's not acting like himself at all, and he took off."

"What's going on?"

"He was so nervous when I last talked to him, and he acted as if he's dodging. I don't know if it's because he was attacked, or something else. I was going to have him stay a few days, but he left. I don't know where he is. I've texted him a couple of times, and he's not responding. I feel like he's hiding something but I don't know what. And I'm worried something might've happened to him. He should call back, and he's not."

"Do you think he knows more about the blackmail than he's telling?"

She sighed heavily. "No. I know you think he's not telling the truth with that, but I think he is. I just don't know what's going on."

"I'm continuing to look. I have a question, though. Does Mowery Transportation give bonuses?"

"Yes, we do. It's based on merit, but also based on the company's performance."

"So someone could get a few thousand dollars?"

"It's possible. Most people probably get between a thousand and two thousand."

"What about five- or ten-thousand dollar bonuses?"

"Frankly, that would just be the higher-ups, and rarely as much as ten thousand. Why?"

"No reason." I decided not to tell her about Hessler just yet.

"What's going on?" she pressed.

"I'll tell you later, okay?" She sighed, and I went on. "Do you know Imperial Supply?"

"That sounds familiar. I think Roger talked about them, but thought they weren't suited for our needs. Why?"

"It came up," I said. "I'll get back to you soon."

"Okay," she said. She sounded disappointed that I didn't have more for her. I was disappointed, too. "If he calls you, will you let me know?"

"Of course," I agreed.

I ended the call and thought for a moment. Where was Dennis? I called him again, and it again went to voice mail. I didn't bother with a message, but texted him and told him it was urgent that I talk to him, and then I went back to my research. I looked up Imperial Supply, found their website, but no mention of Roger. Michelle knew about

Imperial and didn't seem concerned about it, but it would be worth talking to Roger about the company. I made a mental note to follow up with him, and kept working. Holly popped in and out as she helped customers. Cal had sped up a bit, and she filled to-go containers with cupcakes. Her business was doing well. I ran a hand through my hair. "I can't find anything that shows where Clyde Hessler would've come up with thousands of dollars in bonus money," I said. "Enough where he could've bought a truck. New trucks are what, fifty thousand?"

"At least that," Cal said.

"The wife thinks he got a company bonus?" Holly asked.

"Yes," I replied.

"Maybe he's gambling," Holly suggested. "He could be getting cash in smaller amounts that he hoards, and he could tell his wife it was a company bonus."

I mulled on that. "Yeah, that's possible. And Hessler also said that he has access to the petty cash."

"If so, and he really wanted to fool his wife, he could work the books and write himself a company check as a bonus."

"The others in the company obviously haven't watched things that closely," I said.

She shrugged, then headed out front, while Cal continued with his cupcake endeavor. I continued my research. Cal had to help me a time or two, and I found more on Hessler and John Talbot. Unfortunately, however, nothing that helped me. John Talbot appeared clean, nothing suspicious in his financial activities, nothing suspicious from any other standpoint. He had no criminal record, no DUIs or traffic violations, nothing that indicated any kind of trouble. Hessler was the same, except that I couldn't account for any big bonus money, other than the one suspicious deposit from Mowery Transportation. I drummed my fingers on the table and stared at the laptop.

"What's wrong?" Cal asked.

I bit my lip. "It would take some time, but would you be able to run this software and start looking at all of the employees at Mowery Transportation? I've still got a lot of running around to do."

He stopped stirring a new batch of filling. "Sure, but not right away.

I've got to help Holly, and then when I get home, I have some online work for a client. It's probably going to take me all night."

"Whenever you can, just see what you can find."

"Who do you want me to start with?"

I scratched my forehead. "You haven't found anything suspicious with Grant, or Michelle, or Isaac?"

Cal shook his head. "Not so far. I was going to email you a report later. You asked me to look at Christie Costa as well, but I didn't see anything unusual with her, either."

"Okay. Let me know if you see anything else, and look at Ben Mowery and Roger Farley, Michelle's husband. I'll send an email to you with those names. Then go from there."

"You think one of them would blackmail their own relative?" Cal asked as Holly stepped back in.

"Directly, probably not," I said. "But maybe they slipped and revealed something to somebody else at the company. Or, I've thought that someone might've overheard Dennis when he told Talbot what he'd done. Who knows what happened at Mowery Transportation, or what Dennis said?"

Holly frowned as she took the cupcakes Cal had finished and put them into another to-go container. "Don't underestimate anybody. I like to watch some of those true crime shows, like *Dateline* and *20/20*. You'd be surprised, or maybe you wouldn't. Money is a huge motivator. People do an awful lot of bad things for not a lot of money."

I nodded. "Yeah, I've done enough of this to know you're right. That's why I want to look at everybody."

Cal shrugged. "Okay, I'll take care of that later."

I snapped my fingers. "I forgot Warren Singletary."

"Who?" Cal said.

"Someone I saw Dennis with." I told him about Singletary as I worked on the software. "Darn. At first glance, Singletary's finances look normal, although he doesn't have a lot of money. I checked his criminal record as well. He wasn't in any kind of accident, and he hasn't had any DUIs." I hadn't realized I was talking out loud. "When I talked to him, he mentioned some kind of accident, but it doesn't look like he was in one. And Dennis wasn't, either. What was going on there?"

"Sounds like you need to talk to them again," Cal said.

I swore softly. "They're both dodging me." I looked at my watch. It was almost four o'clock. "I've been running around checking other things, and it's time to look at Warren Singletary again."

Cal smiled at me. "You have fun with that. I have more cupcakes to fill."

I grinned at him. "You're doing a great job."

CHAPTER TWENTY-TWO

Warren Singletary didn't answer when I rang the bell. Big surprise. This time, I banged hard on the door a few times. Still no answer.

Was he actually gone?

I narrowed my eyes. I wasn't leaving until I figured out where he was. I went back to my car and parked down the street, then got out and walked around to an alley. It was again cloudy and overcast, and I didn't see anyone. I walked down the alley, past a very friendly dog in another yard who wagged its tail at me but didn't bark, and as I neared the back of Singletary's house, I paused near a dumpster and watched. Singletary's yard was quiet, and I didn't see signs of a dog. I looked around to assure myself I was still alone, then approached a chain-link fence at the corner of the yard. The doghouse sat quietly. I picked up a small rock and threw it at the doghouse. It bounced off with a clunk and landed in the grass. I waited a moment to see what would happen, but no dog appeared. I moved over to a gate and opened it, then stepped cautiously into the yard. I had a better view of the doghouse and could see it was empty. The neighboring houses were quiet as well. I walked up a sidewalk, past the side of the detached garage, and up to the back porch. It was cluttered with an old wooden picnic table, a barbecue, and some old tires and car parts. I stepped past the picnic table and tapped on the back door. No one answered, so I cupped a hand to the glass and peered inside. The kitchen was small, with a round table and chairs, a linoleum floor, dirty dishes on the counter. I didn't see anybody. I tried the knob, but it was locked. I sidled over to a back window and peeked inside. I could see down a gloomy hallway. I moved back to the door and phoned Singletary again, and it still went to voicemail. I'm sure he was tired of my bugging him, and I was tired of calling.

I turned around and surveyed the yard, my frustration building. I quietly walked back to the garage. There was a high window that I couldn't see into. I spied an old metal crate, and I positioned it under the window, hopped on it, and looked in the garage. A covered car sat in the shadows. I hopped off the crate and went to a side door and tried it. It opened. I stepped inside and shut the door, then used my phone flashlight to look around. There was a dusty workbench with tools and a toolbox on it, an old Toro lawnmower and a trimmer, a snowblower and a shovel. I caught a whiff of cut grass. There was plenty of dust on the floor. I stifled a sneeze as I tiptoed to the back end of the car and pulled at the cover, but it was tied down. I got down on my hands and knees and untied a knot, then was able to loosen the cover enough to pull it off the end of the car. I expected to see some classic car, but instead, it was a newer Subaru. I'm not good with cars. I can't tell you the make and model just by looking at one, but I knew enough to know this wasn't any type of special car. I pulled back the cover to expose the back end of the car, but didn't notice anything significant, so I hurriedly removed the entire cover and inspected the car. And then I found it.

The plastic bumper on the front end was damaged on the driver's side. I ran a hand along the metal front panel and noticed a dent as well. I stared at the car for a moment, then took a picture of the license plate. Obviously, the car had been in some kind of accident. But why hadn't I found any indication of Singletary being in an accident when I'd completed a background check on him?

I was still thinking about the car when I heard voices. I quickly stuffed the phone in my pocket and froze. I held my breath and sneaked to the door. I listened for a moment, but couldn't distinguish what the voices were saying. I quietly cracked open the door and peeked out. I could only see into the alley, and no one was there. But the voices were louder, coming from the front of the house. One was Warren. I swore to myself. I didn't want him to know I'd gotten into his garage. Technically it wasn't breaking and entering, because I hadn't broken anything to get in. Maybe trespassing. But I would have explaining that I didn't want to do. I eased the door shut, pulled out my phone, and propped it on the workbench with the flashlight on. Then I hurriedly put the cover back on the car. I hastily tied the knot at the back end, grabbed my phone and shut off the light, and crept back to the door.

I opened it, listened, then poked my head out. No one was in the alley. I looked down the driveway to the front of the house. Warren and another man were standing at the sidewalk, talking. Then they moved out of view. I took the opportunity and stepped out of the garage. I quietly pulled the door shut and dashed back to the gate. I hurried out and latched it, then ran down the alley to the dumpster. My heart was pounding, and I couldn't hear anything else. I let my breathing return to normal as I walked out of the alley. I wished I'd had a chance to look around the garage more, but I definitely found something interesting. I trotted back to my car, got inside, and thought for a moment. I wanted more information on that Subaru, but Cal was busy. I had someone else who could help, though, so I dialed a familiar number.

"Spillman," the voice said.

Detective Sarah Spillman, with the Denver Police Department, and I have been friends for a while now. Well, friends might be a bit of an exaggeration. I'd run into her on a number of investigations, and although she doesn't like my interfering on her turf, she's also begrudgingly accepted that I've helped her on a number of her cases. She also often hints that I may have done some illegal things in order to solve my cases. I would never admit that that's true.

"It's Reed Ferguson," I said.

"Oh. How are you?"

Friendlier than normal. "Fine. How are things with you?"

"Just wrapping up a case. Which, thankfully, means you can't be interfering in it."

I laughed. "Not this time. But I have a favor to ask."

Hesitation. "Oh?"

"Could you look up a license plate for me, find the owner."

"Why?"

"I'm on a new case, trying to find a blackmailer." I explained a little bit about Dennis Mowery. "I'll buy you a cup of coffee."

She sighed heavily. "I probably shouldn't do this, but I expect you'll get the information somewhere anyway. And, in this instance, I can't see how it would hurt." I gave her the license plate number. I heard a phone ring in the background, and she muttered something and said, "That car is registered to Dennis Mowery."

"Really?" I said. "That's strange. Dennis said he'd sold his car a while back."

"Sounds like he lied to you, because the title is still in his name. Or, whoever bought the car never transferred the title."

"Okay. Can you tell whether that car was involved in an accident?"

"Let me check." A pause. "Not that I can see. I hope that helped, but I need to go."

"It did." I thanked her and ended the call.

I put a hand to my chin and stared out the windshield. Why would Dennis have lied to me about selling his car, and why keep the car in Singletary's garage? Unless he was hiding something, like an accident. But the police didn't have an accident report for Dennis's car. Something wasn't adding up, and I was sure Singletary could help with my questions. One thing I did know, he was home, so we were going to have a talk.

I got back out of the 4-Runner and marched around the block to his house. He was still outside talking to his neighbor, and his jaw dropped when he saw me.

CHAPTER TWENTY-THREE

"Hey, Warren," I said pleasantly. "How're you? You've been dodging me."

Singletary glanced nervously at his neighbor. The neighbor, an older man with piercing blue eyes, gazed curiously at Singletary and me. Sweat popped up on Singletary's brow. He looked at his neighbor.

"I'll catch up with you later, okay?"

The man smiled, even though Singletary's tone was gruff. "Sure thing. You take care." He walked off down the street, and Singletary whirled on me.

"What're you doing here?" he hissed.

I shrugged. "I've called you and left messages. Why haven't you answered?"

"Why the hell do you think? I didn't want to talk to you."

I exaggerated a thoughtful nod. "I figured that. Which leaves me no choice. I needed to track you down to talk to you in person." My tone was faux-pleasant now. "You have some explaining to do."

My ringtone started, and I glanced at my phone. Cal was calling. I'd have to talk to him in a minute. I silenced it and looked at Singletary.

He pointed at the phone. "Who was that?"

I wasn't sure if he meant the caller or the ringtone, but I chose the latter. "It's Bogey."

"Huh?"

I shook my head. "It doesn't matter." I crossed my arms. "I see you're storing Dennis's car in your garage."

"I ... don't know what you're talking about."

"Don't lie to me." My amiability vanished in a flash. "I've been running around all day, and I'm fed up."

He looked around and noticed his neighbor still watching. Singletary gestured at the house. "Come with me."

He led me up the sidewalk and into his house. The living room wasn't much, a cheap couch and loveseat pointed at a television hung opposite. The walls were white, the curtains faded, a single painting of a ship in a harbor, the kind you could buy at a hotel art fair. We stood in the shadowy foyer, and Singletary didn't offer for me to take a seat. I smelled cigarette smoke. His studied me guardedly.

"How do you know about the car?" he asked.

"I have my ways." I ran a hand over my eyes. "Warren, level with me. I don't know where Dennis is. He may be in some kind of trouble. Also, someone overheard the two of you talking about an accident, and I saw damage to his car. What happened?"

He ran his tongue over dry lips, then darted into the living room and picked up a pack of cigarettes from a coffee table. He lit one, turned around, and looked at me. His hand shook as he took a drag on it.

"Dennis didn't tell you anything?" he asked.

I shook my head. "I haven't heard from him since this morning, and he's not returning calls. You know someone assaulted him?"

"No."

"Do you know where he is?"

He shook his head, worry creeping into his eyes. "I tried to call him a few times, and he hasn't answered. It's not like him not to call back."

"What are you two afraid of?"

Another drag on the cigarette. His hand still shook. "Dennis will kill me if I tell you," he muttered.

"He might get killed if you don't."

He bit his lip and glanced away. A car went by outside. He looked out the window nervously. Then he finally made a decision.

"I told Dennis when you started asking questions that you were going to figure things out." I didn't say anything, nor did I point out that I hadn't completely "figured things out." But I was pleased that he thought I had. He finally went on. "I've been worrying about this since it happened. I kept telling Dennis that someone was going to trace things back to us. That's why we hid the car."

I stared at him. "You obviously were in an accident. What happened?"

His chin jerked up. "Dennis was the one in the accident. If you want to get technical."

"What happened?" I repeated.

"One night, after Dennis had been fired from Mowery Transportation, he and I went out. We'd been buddies while he was still working at Mowery." A drag on the cigarette. He blew out smoke slowly. "I shouldn't have been drinking, certainly not that much. I could've lost my CDL license. As a matter of fact, I eventually did, but I was worried about it that night. Anyway, Dennis and I had too much to drink. Like usual. We left the bar, and he was taking me back to Mowery where my car was. On the way, we ..." His lower lip trembled as the memory came back to him. "It all happened so fast. It's funny, you can be in a blackout, not remember other things, but I sure as hell remember this."

"What?" I asked softly.

"This guy walked out of nowhere, and Dennis hit him. I don't think the guy died, because Dennis said he looked in the rearview mirror and saw the guy get up. Dennis panicked and kept going, and I told him to stop, but he said he was worried about getting a DUI, that that was the last thing he needed right then. I couldn't convince him to stop, and then I was worried that now I was an accessory. It would cost me my license and my job."

"What happened to the man?"

"We had no idea if he was hurt or not. But we worried that he saw us, and that he'd report us. As I said, Dennis obviously could have been in trouble for drinking and driving, and I was worried I'd get in trouble since I was with him."

"Was there anything in the paper?"

He nodded. "It was on the news, and there was an article about it. The police weren't able to find the car because no one saw us at the time, and all the guy could remember was that it was a newer Subaru. But Dennis and I were in a panic. We went on back to Mowery to get my car, and he followed me to my house. That's when we decided I should keep the car in the garage. It was the middle of the night, and we weren't worried that anybody would see us putting the Subaru there. I got a cover for it, and we left it there. Dennis had been living in his car, so he spent a few nights on my couch. But after a few nights of that, he disappeared." He fidgeted around. "I didn't see him again until recently. He asked about the car, and I told him it was still in the garage, that I've never taken it out. I used to start it, but I haven't in a long time. I hardly even go in the garage, except for the lawnmower or snowblower. Dennis told me he was getting his life together, but he was worried that I'd told somebody about the accident. I kept telling him I didn't, and that it was all okay." He pointed with the cigarette at me. "Until you started asking questions."

It was a lot to digest. I assumed Dennis had been in an accident, but not a hit-and-run. "You really don't know if that person you hit was hurt or killed?"

"I'm sure he was hurt, but I don't know about killed. I never did find anything more about it on the news."

"What was his name?"

He glanced away. "I don't remember."

I could tell he wasn't going to budge on that, so I moved on. "Dennis is worried that somebody knows about it."

"Yes. And maybe that guy found Dennis."

"You think whoever he hit came for him?"

"I don't know, but I think Dennis is scared and disappeared." His voice filled with fear. "If that man found out who hit him, would he come after me, too?"

"How?"

"I don't know. People figure things out, you know?"

I thought for a second. "When you got back to Mowery Transportation the night of the accident, did anybody see you?"

"I don't think so. It was pretty late."

"But Isaac overheard you and Dennis arguing about the accident."

He looked as if he was going to be sick. "Yes. Dennis showed up the next day, and we were talking about it. I told him we should turn ourselves in, and Dennis said no way. We were arguing about that when Isaac heard us. He told Dennis to get out of there. He wasn't very nice to him."

"I heard," I murmured. "Did anybody else overhear you talking about the accident?"

He grimaced. "I don't know." It was almost a wail. "I followed Dennis when he left the property, and we were still talking. Isaac could have told somebody. And so many people come and go; it's hard to say. I saw Dennis later in the day, though. He was hanging around, waiting until after Isaac left. I told him he was taking a chance, and he insisted we had to keep quiet, made me swear that I wouldn't tell anybody." His shoulders sagged. "I haven't told anybody until you."

"Think back. Nobody else saw you later that day?"

He looked to the wall as if picturing what he'd seen. "I know truckers were there, but Isaac's car was gone. Michelle might've been there, but I don't remember."

I assessed the information he'd given me. Learning about the hit-and-run certainly put a wrinkle in things. "And you haven't seen Dennis today?"

Worry etched his face. "No. I hope nothing's happened to him."

I hoped the same thing. But did Dennis's disappearance mean that the blackmailer was back? And had he gone after Dennis? It also could've been that the hit-and-run victim had somehow finally tracked him down.

Singletary finished the cigarette and crushed it out in an ashtray on the coffee table. "Are you going to report Dennis's accident?"

I stared at him. "I don't know yet. Dennis should tell the police, but I don't know if he will."

"Will you?"

I eyed him. "That's the least of your problems. If someone is after the two of you …"

He swore. "Find Dennis, okay? He's my friend." He still looked as if he might be sick.

I nodded and backed out the door. Singletary waited without a word, then closed the door. I called Cal as I walked back to my car.

"Hey, I thought you'd want to know this," he said, so excited he even skipped the "O Great Detective" shtick. "After you left, I started running some checks on the Mowery Transportation employees, like you asked. You'll never guess what I found."

"What?" I got into the 4-Runner.

"A little over a year ago, Ben Mowery made two large deposits into a joint account with his wife. We're talking five grand a couple of times. Cash, not checks."

"Really? Now that's interesting. I know a bank would have to report to the IRS a cash deposit over ten grand. I wonder if Ben was trying to get around that by depositing five thousand twice."

"I don't know, but I thought you'd want to know. I can't find where he's been in any kind of trouble, where he's had other financial issues, that kind of thing. But why would he suddenly have these deposits?"

"Does Ben have other accounts?"

"Yeah, he and his wife also have separate ones. I'm running some reports, but I don't have them yet."

I thought back to my conversation with Ben. He'd been edgy, almost evasive. And when I'd seen him another time, he'd avoided me. Then I thought of something else. He'd said that he led a boring life, always went home at five o'clock. Except that Clyde Hessler had said that he'd seen Ben around the office after hours. Why the discrepancy?

"That's great work, Cal," I said. "Thanks."

"Sure thing. I'm headed home later, and I'll keep at this."

"I appreciate it."

I ended the call but sat for a minute. What was going on with Ben Mowery, and how did it fit into my investigation? I had an inkling of what might be going on, but I needed to verify it. I put the key in the ignition and drove away from Warren Singletary's house.

CHAPTER TWENTY-FOUR

When I arrived at Mowery Transportation, the sun was low in the sky, the heat of the day gone. I parked at the corner, down the street from the gate. I pulled out my binoculars and scanned the property. The warehouses appeared empty, nobody around, big rigs sitting quietly. I turned to look at the main office. Two cars were parked in front, a dark SUV and a red sedan. Ben drove a dark SUV. He'd parked next to me when I'd talked to Isaac Mowery earlier in the day. I didn't recognize the other car.

I watched the office and pondered my next move. The neighborhood was industrial, some businesses still open. A few cars went by, then a black truck, a white SUV, and a delivery truck. Then it grew quiet. Darkness settled in. A dim light went on over the office door. I got out of the 4-Runner, quietly shut the door, and stole across the street. I didn't see anyone as I walked along the sidewalk toward the property gate.

"*Oh, it's not always easy to know what to do.*"

My phone! I swore, both at the noise and at my stupidity for not putting the ringer on silent. Rookie mistake. I hit buttons as I pulled the phone out of my pocket and stopped Bogie from talking. Then I quickly answered.

"Hey Ace, not a good time," I whispered. I looked at the office. No movement.

"Oh, okay," he said, then continued as if it were a perfectly good time to chat. "I just wanted to tell you that Deuce and I talked to Bryce Lindholm and Tony Alvarez. They seem like good guys, and both of them said they were with Taylor Walsh yesterday. They went skiing, then they stopped at Beau Jo's in Idaho Springs for pizza and beers. You know, where all the skiers stop? After that, they went to a bar downtown, and they dropped Taylor off after midnight."

"Did you believe them?" I asked in a low voice. "Anything to make you think they were lying to you?"

"No," he whispered, even though I could hear the sounds of laughter in the background. He and Deuce were probably at B 52s. "Bryce even said they know the waiter at Beau Jo's and that he would vouch for Taylor. I called Beau Jo's and asked the waiter, and he said the guys were there. Was that okay?"

"Yes," I said. "That was great work. You caught me in the middle of something, so I'll talk to you later."

"Okay." He sounded pleased, and I had to admit that the Goofballs had again done a good job.

I ended the call, silenced the phone, and stuffed it back in my pocket. As I walked along the sidewalk, I studied the office building. I couldn't see any, but I was sure there were security cameras. I didn't know if they'd catch me at the gate. I shrugged to myself. I'd explain myself to Michelle later. I wanted to confirm something now.

I stopped near the gate. A chain and padlock held it closed. I looked around to make sure I was alone. I debated whether to climb over the fence, and then I noticed the padlock. It held the chain together, but it wasn't locked. Was that an indication of bad security, or was someone still inside? I grabbed the padlock and quietly opened it, then slipped it off the chain. I eased open the gate, cringing when the hinges squeaked. I looked to the office building, but no one came out. I slipped onto the property, closed the gate, and put the padlock back in place. Then I ran over to one of the big rigs and ducked down. I peeked around it toward the warehouses and listened. I didn't see or hear anyone. I turned back to the main office. A few lights shown from windows, but I didn't hear anything. A lone car passed on the street, and I scooted around to the front of the truck. The car slowed down and for a panicky moment, I thought it was stopping at the gate. But it drove to the corner and paused at a stop sign, then moved on. I hadn't realized I was holding my breath, until I let it out.

I finally hurried up to the front of the office building and peeked into the windows of both vehicles. I couldn't see much inside either one, so I dashed toward the corner of the building. I couldn't tell if any security cameras would pick up my presence. My heart pounded as I again listened. Just street noises. I glanced along the side of the building. There were several windows, and dim light filtered from one of them. I sneaked along the wall toward it and paused underneath. I thought I heard voices, but I couldn't be sure. I raised up on tiptoes, but the window was too high for me to look in. I swore silently. I looked around, but didn't see a crate, box, or anything that I could stand on. I again thought I heard noises. I moved around to the back of the building. A chain-link fence was nearby, but nothing to help me look in the window. I sidled back along the side of the building toward the front, and then I was sure I heard a noise. I froze for a moment, then realized somebody was out front. I slipped to the corner and peeked around.

Christie Costa was standing in a halo of light in the doorway, looking back into the building. Her hair was tousled, and she tugged down a short skirt. She smiled and said something I couldn't understand.

"This has to stop," a low voice said.

"I know," she replied.

"You go on home. I'll lock up in a minute."

She disappeared from view, then came back outside. She quietly shut the office door and walked to her car. She started it, backed up, and drove to the gate. She got out, seemingly unconcerned about anyone watching her, and slipped the open padlock off the chain. She drove her car off the property, hopped out and slid the padlock back in place, and returned to her car. Then her red taillights disappeared down the street.

It grew quiet again. I stayed close to the building and eased up to the front door. I tried the knob, and it turned. I opened the door and quickly stepped inside. It took a moment for my eyes to adjust to the dim light. The room was empty, but light shone down the hallway. I heard noises. I raced across the main room and looked quickly down the hall, then ducked my head back as Ben walked out of his office. He was adjusting his shirttails with one hand, and he held something in the other. He walked down the hall and opened a door. A light came on as he stepped inside. I moved down the hall as quietly as I could and looked at the door. The men's room. I pushed the door open just a crack, and froze when I saw Ben standing at the sink brushing his teeth. I let the door quietly shut before he saw me, then moved down the hall to another doorway. A moment later, Ben emerged from the bathroom and headed back to his office. Did he know I was there? He went inside and I crept back down the hall. His door was propped open, and I stopped when I heard his voice. For a second, I thought he was talking to me. Then I realized I was wrong.

"Hey, honey, sorry I got tied up again." A pause. "No, it's just another inspection that we're not quite ready for. I know, it's been hectic. But it'll be over soon. I'll be home in a little while, okay?"

I heard the sound of a phone receiver clicking down. I tiptoed closer and looked in. Ben was straightening the desktop, putting his monitor back in place, centering the keyboard. Then he sat down, put his elbows on the desk, and put his head in his hands.

I moved into the doorway and leaned against the door jamb. "Don't like lying to your wife?" I asked.

His head jerked up and he swore when he saw me.

CHAPTER TWENTY-FIVE

Ben's jaw worked and finally words came out. "What the hell are you doing here?"

I smiled at him. "You shouldn't leave the front door unlocked. People could walk right in."

Ben put a hand to his chest, then sat down. "I don't feel so good."

I stepped into the room, worried he was having a heart attack. "Are you okay?"

He sat back and his hand dropped into his lap. "I should call the police, report you for breaking and entering."

I shook my head. "I didn't break in. I told you, you left the door unlocked."

He swore softly. "What do you want?"

I glanced around his office. A couple of pictures of big rigs hung on the walls, similar to Grant's office, and a few metal file cabinets sat in a corner. A framed photo of Ben and a similarly aged woman sat on his desk. I pointed to it.

"Your wife?"

His face colored. "None of your business."

I took a chair across from his desk without being asked. I casually crossed one leg over the other and contemplated him. "Did you have a good time with Christie?"

He tried to keep a straight face as he drew in a careful breath. "What're you talking about?"

I closed my eyes and fought to keep my temper in check. "Geez, is everybody going to try lying to me?"

"I don't know ..." His voice trailed off.

"I had a suspicion you were up to something," I said. "I wasn't quite able to put it all together until I found out that you've had a couple of large deposits to your bank account."

"How do you know that?" he asked, then frowned when he realized he'd said too much.

I waved a dismissive hand. "I have my ways. Then someone said they'd seen your car here late at night." I pointed at him. "But you specifically told me you always go home at five." I glanced at the picture of his wife again. "That's not true, now, is it?"

His mouth worked as he considered what to say. "It's not what you think," was all he finally managed.

I lowered my voice a notch. "Oh, I think it's exactly what I think." Then I made a face, wondering if I'd made sense.

He shook his head. "You're not going to tell anyone?"

"That depends. Want to fill me in on the details?"

He seemed to shrink in the chair. "I never meant for it to happen."

"They never do," I murmured.

He glared at me and repeated, "It's not what you think. My wife and I have been drifting apart for a long time. We don't have any kids, and I don't know what I'm going to do when I retire. I'm not sure I want to, but Grant has been hinting that I should hang it up. He thinks I can't keep up with everything like I used to." He got a faraway look. "Then one day a while back I noticed Christie. She looked really good, and she was so friendly to me. It hit me just at the wrong time, when my wife and I were just ... I don't know, strangers in the same house. I knew I shouldn't have done anything, but I swear, Christie came after me."

It was my turn to shake my head. "Oh, please. Don't blame her. You were weak."

He sighed heavily. "Okay, maybe I was. It just happened one evening. I was about to leave for the day, and she asked me for some help with a report I'd given her. We chatted about that for a few minutes, and then I left. But, I could tell, she was flirting with me. It happened again a week later, and this time, we stayed a little longer. I didn't think anyone was around, and we ended up back in my office. Then, well, you know ..."

"How often did this happen?"

"Not that many times," he said defensively.

"When Dennis was still working here?"

He frowned. "Yeah, a time or two."

I stared at him. "And let me guess, one night while you and Christie were here, you overheard Dennis talking to someone about some skimming he was doing. What did you do with that knowledge?"

He bolted forward in the chair, hands on the desk. "No, that's not true. I didn't know anything about what Dennis was doing. You think I would blackmail my own nephew?"

I put my fingertips together as I stared at him. "Quite frankly, I don't know what to think. I've got a list of suspects longer than my arm. Someone had to have known what Dennis was up to. And Dennis thinks someone overheard him when he was here one night. Maybe you were here at the same time?"

He gritted his teeth, his jaw muscles tight. He swore at me. "You have no idea what you're talking about."

"Then tell me where I'm wrong. Tell me what you know."

He slapped the desk angrily. "You really missed the boat, you know?"

I put my hands down. "How?"

He settled down a bit, then ran a hand over his face. "Dennis isn't the only one being blackmailed."

I raised my eyebrows. "You?"

"Yeah, me, too." His voice was small. "I thought I'd gotten away with it, because Christie and I weren't meeting that often. But then a couple of weeks ago, I got a note. It was typed up, and said they knew about the affair. If I didn't pay up, they would tell Grant and Michelle." He threw up his hands. "What was I supposed to do? I can't let them know about this. Not only would I be humiliated, it would wreck my relationships with everyone."

"What about Christie?"

"Yeah, it would hurt her, too. She'd lose her job."

He didn't seem that concerned about her.

"Do you still have the note?"

He shook his head. "I burned it."

Too bad. "How much did they want?"

"Ten grand."

"How did you deliver the money?"

He pushed a pen back and forth on the desk. "I had to go to Ashbaugh Park. It's near my house. I was to put the money in a trash can near a certain bench near the pond and then leave. That was all."

"How many times did this happen?"

"Once. I did as I was told, and I left."

"You didn't wait around to see who would pick up the money?"

He shook his head. "No. The note said that if I stayed around, that they'd tell everyone." He swallowed hard. "I couldn't risk it. I naïvely thought if I paid up, that would be the end, but then I got another note. They wanted another ten thousand."

"When did you deliver that?"

He shook his head. "I haven't. It's supposed to be tomorrow night."

"Where?"

"The same place. It's exactly the same."

I stared at him in disbelief. "So you're being blackmailed, and you continue the relationship with Christie? I don't want to offend you, but that seems really stupid."

"You don't understand. Christie and I have been on-again off-again for a long time. Just when I think we've moved on, I see her here, and there's tension between us. Mostly I've ignored it, but sometimes …" He shrugged. "But after I got that note and paid up, I told myself it had to stop."

"But it obviously didn't. Does she know about the blackmail?"

"No. I *did* tell her we needed to stop seeing each other, and I thought that would be the end of it. But she told me today that she needed to talk. I didn't know what it was about." He looked down. "I think I hurt her, and I don't blame her. I wanted to somehow make it right. We agreed to meet for dinner, and we went to a restaurant near here. We talked, and I told her we shouldn't see each other anymore, that we couldn't go on like this. She said she understood, and then we came back here." The pen stopped moving. He sighed. "We came inside, just to talk. But damn, she looked so good. One thing led to another, and ..." He glared at me. "Do I have to paint you a picture?"

"I get the idea," I said. "I am going to say it again. How stupid."

He didn't dare argue with that. "I've got myself into quite a situation."

"I can't disagree." I thought for a moment. "Someone saw the two of you together, either in the middle of it, or they knew enough to know what you were doing. *I* was suspicious. You never saw or heard anything?"

"No," he said with emphasis. "Do you think either one of us would be that stupid if we thought somebody was around?"

Did he actually ask that question? I wasn't going to comment on how smart or stupid he was. "Think back to the times you were with her. Did you hear anything, see anyone when you went outside? A car that shouldn't be there, something like that?"

He shook his head, and when I stared at him, he thought longer. "No, I'm sorry. I thought we were being cautious."

"You never saw Dennis around when you were here with Christie?"

"No. He was so drunk half the time I never would've worried about it."

"Was Isaac around when you were with Christie?" I asked.

"No. He's out in the warehouse or he goes home. Everybody always left."

I mulled over everything he'd said. "You took an awfully big risk."

"I know," he whispered.

"What about your wife? How come she never got suspicious?"

"She doesn't know what goes on around here. She lost interest in my work a long time ago, does her own thing. She quit coming to the company functions, and she doesn't even know Christie, other than occasionally talking to her on the phone when she needs to talk to me.

If I had to work late, I would just tell her I had an inspection or something like that. She didn't care."

There was just a hint in his tone that maybe I should feel sorry for him. I didn't.

"What about the deposits into your joint account? That was over a year ago. That made me wonder if you were the blackmailer."

He shook his head in disgust. "My wife got an inheritance. The money went into her account, but then we transferred some to our joint account."

"A cash deposit?" I was skeptical.

He shrugged. "It's two different banks, and I didn't want to hassle with a cashier's check, and I was in a hurry. Besides, I was going right from one bank to the other."

I wasn't sure I bought that, but I could track it down. "Let's go back to the blackmail drop. It's tomorrow night?"

He nodded. "The same deal as before."

I thought for a second. "I need to be there."

"Why?" He was scared.

"Because whoever is blackmailing you almost assuredly was blackmailing Dennis. I've been at a dead end trying to find out who it is. But now we can set a trap for them."

He mumbled something, then said, "You won't tell anybody about this, will you?"

I looked at him drily. "I won't. But, truth is, it's going to come out at some point. It's probably better that it come from you than me."

He looked away. "You're right. I should've known it would come to this."

"Do you know where Dennis is? Have you heard from him?"

He shook his head. "I've only seen him a couple of times since he's resurfaced, but we haven't talked much."

"I want him at the blackmail drop tomorrow, if I can find him. He went through the same thing."

"You'll tell Dennis what I did?" He didn't like that. "You really think that's necessary?"

"I do." I shifted in my chair. "But I have to find him first." Something suddenly occurred to me, something that I'd missed before. I had an idea where Dennis might be.

"What do we do now?" he finally asked.

"I need to plan out a few things for tomorrow night." I stood up. "Let's go."

CHAPTER TWENTY-SIX

Ben walked me to the door and looked out cautiously. I stared at him.

"You've already been caught," I said.

He shrugged. "I suppose you're right." He sounded defeated. "You said you want Dennis at the blackmail drop tomorrow night. How are you going to find him?"

Something had occurred to me while I'd been talking to Ben. "I think I know where he is. You wait for my call, and I'll fill you in." I was about to step out the door, but I stopped. "How did you explain it to your wife the last time you had to drop the money off?"

He smiled. "Everybody thinks I just go home and stay there, but I don't. Sometimes I stop at a little bar around the corner for a drink or two. My wife doesn't care. She has her friends, and does her thing."

It sounded like a sad marriage, and I was thankful Willie and I got along well. And then my heart leaped in my throat for a second as I thought about possibly losing her. That couldn't happen. No way.

"Don't mention tomorrow night to anybody," I said. "The last thing we want to do is scare off the blackmailer."

He nodded. "I'll keep my mouth shut. You don't have to worry."

That I believed. He was frightened and didn't want anybody to know what he'd been up to. Unfortunately for him, as well as everyone else involved, all this was going to come out.

"Let me get the gate," he said.

"Why didn't you lock it before?"

He jerked at thumb at his chest. "The last one out locks it."

I stepped outside and Ben crossed the lot and undid the padlock on the gate. He waited until I walked out, and he sighed as he put the chain back on. By the time I got to my car, he was back inside the building. I drove away, but I didn't go home. It didn't take me very long to get back to Warren Singletary's neighborhood. I parked down the street and watched his house. A light shone from the front window. I got out and walked to his house, but didn't bother ringing the bell. Instead, I crept quietly around the side of the house and up to the detached garage. I peered into the back yard and listened. Still no dog around. Singletary might've had a dog in the past, but not now. If so, he'd probably kept the doghouse just to scare off intruders. Like me. Still, I waited. I didn't hear a dog or anyone else. I stole quietly over to the side door of the garage and put my hand on the knob. Then I quickly opened the door.

Dennis was sitting in the back seat of the Subaru, illuminated by his phone flashlight, which was sitting on the seat next to him. He had a Subway sandwich halfway to his mouth, and he dropped it in his lap. His eyes went wide.

"What're you doing here?"

I stepped inside and shut the door, then leaned back and crossed my arms. "I could ask you the same thing."

He recovered quickly and put the sandwich on a wrapper. "I needed a place to stay. Warren hardly ever comes in here, and I knew I'd likely be safe for a few days. How did you know?" He grabbed a napkin.

I glanced around. "I was in here earlier today, and I found your car. But it didn't hit me right away that something was off." I pointed to the floor. "The dust. It's all over the garage, and it should have been all over the cover on the car, too. But when I moved the cover earlier, there was no dust on it. Like I said, I didn't think about it right away, not until I talked to your uncle."

Even in the dim light, I could see his face get whiter. A bruise from his assault was pronounced. "Why were you talking to my uncle?"

I stared at him. "Because he's being blackmailed, too."

He stopped wiping his hands on the napkin. "What did he do?"

"He's having an affair." I told him what I'd discovered about Ben. When I finished, he shook his head sadly.

"For the last several years, I didn't think Ben was very happy. It's too bad for him, but he shouldn't have done that with Christie."

I gestured at the front of the car. "Warren told me about your accident."

"Yeah, he broke down, didn't he?"

I ignored that. "You told me you sold the car."

"Well, I lied."

"I see why. You didn't want to tell me?"

"Of course not. I didn't know what you'd do if you did find out. Have you told anyone?"

"Not yet." I stared at him. "When you were beat up, the guy said stop digging into the past?"

"Something like that."

"Would that mean the hit-and-run?"

"I don't know. I've worried since the accident happened that Warren wouldn't be able to keep his mouth shut." He groaned.

I put a hand to my nose to keep from sneezing. "You should give him some credit. He didn't tell anybody until he told me."

"You believe him?"

I nodded. "Yeah, I do. He doesn't want anybody to know he was with you that night. He has plenty of reasons to keep quiet now that you've both covered up a crime."

He cleared his throat. "I feel terrible about that. When that guy darted into the street, I could hardly react before I hit him. It was awful, but I wasn't thinking straight at all. All I knew is that I didn't want to get caught, didn't want to get into any trouble. I'd go to jail."

"What happened after you left Michelle's this morning?"

"I was scared, man." He sneered. "It's obvious someone's after me, and I don't know if it's because of you poking around, or if the person I hit with the car finally figured out who I am."

"How would they do that?"

He shrugged. "I don't know. But you managed to track me down now, so someone else could have, too."

"Is that why you were nervous when we first talked? You were holding back. You didn't want me to find out about the accident."

"Yeah, man. If you were digging around about the blackmail, what else would you find?"

"But if the guy you hit figured out it was you, wouldn't he turn you in to the police?"

"Maybe he figured it would be hard to prove his case. I don't know. I was scared, and I wasn't going to stay at Michelle's any longer. Roger doesn't like me, and he's really pissed since he found out I stole from the company."

"Can you blame him?"

His chin shot up. "I'm going to make things right. Somehow I'm going to pay back the money I took."

"Why is Isaac so angry with you?"

"It's always been that way, and it didn't help that I showed up after I'd been fired. He wondered what I was up to. And as you say," he said starkly, "can you blame him?"

I thought for a second. "Someone started blackmailing you shortly after the Broncos-Bears game on a Monday night. Your friend John remembered that that game was on when you called him, and you were pretty drunk, I guess. Do you recall that?" He shook his head, and I went on. "He says you were going on about stealing from your company, skimming money off to pay for drugs."

He nodded. "So?"

"Talbot could be our blackmailer. Or he told someone about what you were doing."

He twisted up his lip. "I guess so, but John wasn't like that. He's a nice guy."

"Maybe." I went on. "What about the hit-and-run?" He shrugged. "If you're not going to be honest with people, it's going to eat away at you." He didn't say anything. "You need to let Michelle know you're okay."

He nodded slowly. "I will."

"And we need to see if we can find this blackmailer."

"How?"

"I have an idea."

Just then, the garage door opened and hit me in the back side.

"Dennis!" Singletary poked his head in. He saw me and swore. "What's going on?"

I stepped aside and he came in and shut the door.

"Sorry, Warren," Dennis said. "I needed a place to crash, and I knew you don't come out here much."

Singletary exchanged a glance with me, then said to Dennis, "Yeah, man, it's okay. I wish you would've told me."

Dennis shrugged. "I didn't want you to get into any trouble."

"It's okay." Singletary looked at me. "You don't give up, do you?"

I shook my head. "I needed to find Dennis. We've got some things to iron out."

"Oh," Singletary said. He looked at Dennis. "You want to sleep in the house?"

Dennis nodded. "Yeah. I'll come in later."

Singletary stared at him, then realized he was being dismissed. "Okay, I'll see you in a bit." He gave me a curt nod and backed out the door.

"Watch out for the dog," I said.

"What dog?" Singletary replied. Then, "Oh, yeah. I don't have one anymore."

"Right," I said slowly.

Singletary glared at me and left. I turned back to Dennis. "Here's what we need to do."

I detailed my plans to Dennis, and then I left.

When I got home, Willie was in bed. Humphrey slept near her head, and he meowed at me. I scratched his belly and was rewarded with some loud purring. Then I undressed and crawled in next to Willie. She woke up and turned to me.

"You okay?" I asked.

"Yes. Don't worry about me."

Easier said than done. She asked about my day, and I quickly filled her in. Then I held her close, and we drifted off to sleep.

CHAPTER TWENTY-SEVEN

The next day I spent a while putting some plans into effect. It was Friday, and I knew the Goofballs would be available that night. I talked to them, and then I called Cal. He wasn't thrilled with my request, but he agreed to help. Willie, however, bowed out. I couldn't blame her.

At eleven o'clock, Dennis and I were in the 4-Runner, parked down the block from Ashbaugh Park, a large park with a pond near Santa Fe and Mineral. It was quiet, and the park was closed. A shadow approached, and I realized it was Ben. He hopped in the car.

"How'd it go?" I asked.

"I put the money in the trash can, and I walked back to my car and drove a few blocks away. Then I walked back here, just like you told me to."

"Good," I said.

"Did anyone see you?" Dennis asked.

Ben shook his head and looked at me. "Do you think this is going to work?"

I shrugged as I trained my binoculars on the park. I couldn't see the trash can. "Let's hope so."

My phone rang, and I put it on speaker. Ben glanced at me, amused by the ring tone. I suppose Ben was old enough at least to recognize the voice.

"Reed, Ace and I are in position," Deuce said.

"Great," I replied. "What do you see?"

Earlier that day, I'd worked with them on the plan. They'd been waiting on the other side of the park for an hour, in a spot where they could see anyone approaching the trash can. Cal and Holly were in his car at another area. He was videotaping the area near the trash can. I felt as if my bases were covered. When somebody came to get the money, one of us, at least, would see them.

"Keep an eye out," I said to Deuce, "and if you see anybody, call me."

"You got it."

"Do you think he'll show up?" Dennis asked.

I didn't say anything for a moment. "We'll find out."

We sat quietly and waited. I'd cracked the windows, but I couldn't risk discovery, so I had the engine off. Which meant no air conditioning. And it was still warm. Both Dennis and Ben were fidgety, moving around a lot. I finally scolded them both to stay still. The minutes ticked by, and the park remained quiet. My phone rang again.

"Yeah?" I said.

Cal's nasally voice came through the phone. "I'm not seeing anything over here. What about you?"

I shook my head. "Nothing so far."

"What if your guy doesn't show?"

"Let's give it a little longer."

"Okay." He sounded chipper. Probably enjoying time with Holly. I wasn't putting him in any danger. The Goofballs' greatest fear when they helped me was being bored, but Cal's greatest worry was being put in danger. I assured him nothing would happen. And it looked as if that would be the case. Several more minutes dragged by, and then I called Cal back.

"I don't think it's happening."

"No, but should we give it a little longer?"

I agreed, but after another fifteen minutes, and a couple of phone calls to him and the Goofballs, we gave up. Ben, Dennis, and I got out of the car and walked to the park. Ace, Deuce, Holly, and Cal joined us by the trash can, which really needed to be emptied. Ben turned his head and held his breath, then reached inside and pulled out a small bag.

"Do you think he knew we were watching him?" Ben asked.

"I think that's obvious," I said in a low voice. I studied him. "You're sure you didn't tell anybody about this?"

"No!" he said. "I kept my mouth shut."

"Somebody figured it out," Ace said innocently.

"I didn't say anything," Ben repeated.

Dennis began pacing. "I swear, whoever this is, they've ruined our lives." He whirled around. "Ben, what did you do today?"

"Keep your voices down," I said.

Ben thought for a second. "I stayed outside in the warehouses. I didn't want to see anybody in the office, especially Christie."

"And you didn't talk to anyone about tonight?" Cal asked.

He shook his head. "I'm telling you guys, I kept my mouth shut."

I looked to Dennis. "This was similar to your blackmail drop, correct?"

He kept pacing. "Yes. I was told to give an envelope with the money to Taylor."

"And Taylor put the money in a crate near the dumpster behind Billy's restaurant," I said.

"I don't understand tonight, though," Dennis went on. "The blackmailer got cold feet, I guess."

I looked at all of them. "What did everyone see? Anybody walking around, a car going by?"

Cal shook his head, but Deuce held up a hand. "A dark truck drove by us a while ago, but it just went on past. I didn't think anything of it." Ace nodded agreement.

"A dark truck?" I thought for a minute, putting some pieces together. "Clyde Hessler drives a dark truck."

I turned to Ben and Dennis. "I've been suspicious of him. Any chance he knew what the two of you were doing?"

Ben pursed his lips. "I don't know. He mostly keeps to himself. How would he have found out?"

Dennis nodded. "Clyde didn't like me."

"I hate to break it to you," Ben said quietly, "but not many people did. Not with your drinking and belligerent behavior. Hell, Roger would complain to me about you, said that –"

"Roger doesn't like anybody in the family," Dennis interrupted. "He thinks he's better than the rest of us, has his eyes and ears on everything that goes on at the company, and he's nosy as hell. He has a chip on his shoulder, and –"

I held up a hand to stop Dennis. "Hold on. What did you say?"

Dennis stared at me. "Roger's a jerk. He keeps tabs on everything, just looking to get people in trouble."

My mind raced. "Clyde said something similar, about how Roger was all over the place, keeping tabs on everything." Had I been looking at this all wrong? "Cal. You said Roger Farley was involved in a bad business deal, correct?"

Cal nodded. "Yeah, it looks as if he'd lost money on it, but I didn't find a lot of details."

"What if he needs money because of that?" I said to no one in particular. I received a collective shrug. "I think we need to focus on Roger again."

CHAPTER TWENTY-EIGHT

I looked at Ben and Dennis. "How much do you know about Roger's finances over the years?"

Ben shrugged. "I don't know. He doesn't say a whole lot about things like that."

I thought for a second. "Clyde didn't think Roger was happy working at Mowery Transportation. Roger even said that he'd wanted to branch out on his own."

"That's not a big secret," Dennis said. "Roger's always wanted to do more, and has always hinted that the family hasn't let him. To be honest, he's been kind of snide about Michelle, and I haven't appreciated it."

Ben nodded. "Yes, that's true. I always thought we were doing a good thing to give Roger the work, the opportunity. I thought that's what he wanted, but over the years, he's made it sound like we forced him into it." He sighed. "He could've done his own thing any time he wanted, or at least any time he had the means to try."

Dennis shook his head. "I hate to say it, but I don't think Michelle would've wanted that. She's always wanted the business to stay in the family."

Ace and Deuce were both getting squirmy, shifting from foot to foot. I glanced at them.

"Why don't you two head home?" I suggested. I clapped Ace on the shoulder and nudged Deuce. "Thanks for coming out to help. I might have to put you on the payroll."

They both laughed at that, then waved at everyone and headed out of the park.

I thought about everything Ben and Dennis had told me, then looked at Cal. "I want to dig deeper into Roger's stuff. Can you help?"

He nodded. "Sure." Then he looked a little uncertain. "I was going to go to Holly's now."

"Oh," I said. "I don't want to interrupt."

Holly smiled. "You're both welcome at the house. I'm tired and I'm going straight to bed because I have to work tomorrow. But you two can work if you want."

"We'll be quiet," Cal said.

Ben glanced at his watch. "I need to get home. I'm never out this late, and Sheryl will be asking."

He looked nervous at the prospect of going home, and I was sure he was thinking about how he was going to explain things – such as his affair – to his wife. Dennis nodded at him.

"Could you give me a ride back to Warren's house?"

"Sure," Ben said.

They both gave me a halfhearted wave.

"Let us know what you find out," Ben said to me.

"Keep your mouths shut," I warned them. "If Roger is the blackmailer, we don't want him to know we're on to him."

"You don't have to worry about that," Dennis said.

I got Ben's number so I could touch base with him later. "And if you hear anything from the blackmailer, call me right away."

"I will."

He and Ben started down the street. When they were gone, I turned to Holly and Cal.

"We should head out now before we attract attention."

Holly smiled. "We'll see you back at my house."

I thanked them and hurried back to the 4-Runner. I was tempted to call Willie to tell her that I'd be even later than I'd originally thought, but decided not to. When she'd come home from work this evening, she was tired. I hoped she was getting some rest. I started the car and drove past Ashbaugh Park. I was disappointed that the evening had been a bust. But, if Roger was the blackmailer, I hoped to figure that out.

I drove north to Sixth, then west into Golden, where Holly lived in a small frame house off Washington Street. When I got there, Cal's beat-up Honda Civic was parked in front. A light was on in the front window of the house. I walked up the porch steps, and Cal opened the door.

"I saw you drive up," he said. "Come on in."

I stepped into a living room decorated with a tan couch and loveseat with purple throw blankets, and maple coffee and end tables. It was cute, warm and comfortable, and a bit old-fashioned, and Cal seemed right at home. Holly popped her head in from the kitchen.

"I have some cupcakes if you want them. They're a day old, but they still taste good."

Cal nodded. "Yes, they do. And the filling is especially good!"

"I'd love one," I said.

Holly disappeared and came back with two chocolate cupcakes. "Help yourself. I've got to be at the shop early tomorrow, so I'm going to bed." She pointed to a laptop on the coffee table. "Reed, feel free to use that, if you need to."

"Thanks, and I appreciate your letting me invade your space," I said.

"Any time." She waved, kissed Cal, and went down a hallway. Cal watched her, contentment all over his face.

"You're falling in love, aren't you?" I asked after I heard her door shut.

He didn't say anything, but moved over to a small folding table that had been set up next to the couch, a makeshift work area for him. He had a couple of monitors set up, his laptop already hooked up to them. He sat down at the laptop and gestured for me to take the couch. I plopped down, and I looked at him. He was staring at the computer, not typing yet. Then he spoke softly.

"I think I am. Reed, did you ever think this would happen to me?"

I didn't answer right away, then I shook my head. "I really never did. You've always seemed content to be alone, the introvert. Safe in your home in the mountains, working online. Rarely socializing. Holly has brought out a different side of you, and it's great."

He smiled. "Yeah, it is." Then he switched gears. "Let's see what we can find on Roger Farley."

I shifted on the couch, put an elbow on the arm, and watched Cal work.

"We know he was involved in this recent business dealing," I began.

"Right," Cal said. "Let me look at a few more things."

I borrowed Holly's laptop to do my own research on Roger. The room was quiet, both of us working silently. I couldn't find any social media sites for Roger, but I did stumble across Michelle's Facebook page, and then I found Andy's and Jordan's. Nothing seemed noteworthy. Then Cal spoke up.

"I'm looking at Roger's business, Imperial Supply. Something doesn't add up. I thought he'd invested in the company, but it looks like he owns it. He's been careful, though, made it hard to tie ownership back to him."

"So that Michelle and the family wouldn't know?"

"Could be." He paused. "Let's check the company's bank account." Another pause. "It looks like some bills are overdue." He worked some more. "And here's something else," Cal said, his voice low with concern. "I've been going back further, and Roger was involved in another deal about sixteen months ago." He frowned with distaste. "The same bank account. Amateur."

I sat up. "Sixteen months ago? That's about the time that Dennis was blackmailed."

He nodded. "There's two big deposits here, one for ten thousand and one for twenty. Cash."

I thought over everything I knew. "Dennis paid the blackmailer about those same amounts."

Cal kept working, but didn't divulge any more. I finally yawned and stretched. "I can't do these all-nighters like you," I said. "I need to go home and get some sleep."

He laughed softly. "I'm used to it. It's my best time to work." He tapped the monitor. "I'll keep looking at this. If there's more, I want to find it."

"I appreciate the help."

"You know I love this part. And I'm glad things at the park weren't dangerous."

I saw a twinkle in his eye. "You and Holly had fun."

"Yeah, we did. Holly thought she would be bored, but she said she enjoyed spending time with me."

"It's nice to have someone say that, right?"

He reddened. "Yeah, it is."

I set Holly's laptop on the coffee table and got up. "I better get home."

"Tell Willie hello." He glanced at me. "Is everything okay?"

With all that had been going on, I hadn't told Cal about Willie. I did so now. I knew she'd probably prefer I didn't, but I really needed to say it to somebody. He blinked a few times when I finished.

"Reed, I'm so sorry." I nodded, and he went on. "You two are family. If there's anything I can do ..."

I gulped back my fear. "Yeah, I know. It's going to be okay."

"Yeah," he forced some cheer. "It will. You'll see. She'll get the mammogram blah results, and it'll be fine." He bit his lip, unsure what to say. "Keep me posted."

I thanked him and quietly let myself out. The street was silent as I headed to Washington Street and turned onto Sixth Avenue. It was after two in the morning, but there was still a decent number of cars on the road. As Denver has grown, so has its traffic. I was tired, and only when I got to Broadway and then drove into my own neighborhood did I notice a set of headlights behind me. Was I being followed? I sped down the wrong block and around a corner, and the car stayed with me. Then I turned on my street and drove slowly as I looked for a parking place. Behind me, the headlights moved on, but I was concerned. I parked down the block and walked back to my building. It was quiet, no lights on in the Goofballs' condo, none at mine, either. I walked around the side of the building and up the steps, and quietly let myself in. I got a drink of water in the kitchen and padded into the bedroom. Both Humphrey and Willie were sleeping. I was too wound up, so I watched *In A Lonely Place*, since I hadn't been able to talk Willie into watching it with me the other night. No matter how many times I've seen it, I always love to watch it again. Always seeing a little something new in the Dixon Steele character. Always a renewed appreciation for Bogart's acting skills. And despite the film's dark mood, it helped me to relax. After that, I was finally tired, so I crept into the bedroom and tried not to disturb Humphrey and Willie as I got into bed. I quickly fell asleep.

CHAPTER TWENTY-NINE

When I woke up the next morning, Willie was still asleep. I laid in bed and thought about my investigation. Roger Farley was my number one suspect; I had a bad feeling about him. But I didn't have any actual proof he was a blackmailer, and I wasn't ready to confront him just yet.

Willie stirred, yawned, and looked at me. "Good morning."

"Hey," I said. "How're you doing?"

"You got home late." Humphrey jumped up on her lap.

"Yeah, I didn't want to wake you." I stared at her.

She shrugged. "I'm okay. I keep telling myself that whatever's going on with me is nothing, but I don't know. I have a bad feeling about this."

She held Humphrey, and he purred in her arms. I reached over and took her hand.

"Let's don't get ahead of ourselves here. One thing at a time. Whatever happens, we'll get through this together. I love you."

"I love you, too."

She kissed me, then sighed heavily. "Darcy and I are going out today, to take my mind off things. I figured you'd be tied up."

"Good guess. I have a lot to do."

I filled her in on my case, and then I asked about her work. She told me about one of her coworkers who liked to tell funny stories, and I smiled as she relaxed a bit. Then we got up. While she showered, I checked my email. Cal had found more information on Roger's company, Imperial Supply. The company was in trouble and was hemorrhaging money. Cal sent some financials, then wrote that he'd been up most of the night and he was sleeping now while Holly was at work. Humphrey came into the room and meowed. I picked him up as I mulled over my next move. Since Willie was spending the day with Darcy, I decided to see what Roger was up to. I called Michelle Farley first.

"Reed, do you have any update?"

"Not yet. Have you heard from Dennis?"

"Yes. He was vague, but said he's all right. I don't like it, though. Something's going on."

"Hmm." I played dumb. "I'll see if I can talk to him. How're things at your house?"

"Fine. Just a lazy Saturday morning." But she didn't sound okay. She sounded worried. "Roger and I are going out later, but if you need to talk to me, call. Oh, and I checked on Christie Costa. She hasn't been paid any overtime."

"Okay, good." It was a moot point now, but I didn't tell her that. Humphrey was needy and didn't want me talking on the phone. He kept batting at my hands and meowing. "I'll update you soon. Thanks." I tried to appease Humphrey with a cat toy while I called Ben Mowery. He answered tentatively.

"Oh, Reed, it's you."

"Yeah, maybe you should save my number, save me from having to come knock on your door."

"Okay, I will."

"Have you heard anything more from the blackmailer?" I asked as I dangled the feather-on-a-stick for Humphrey.

"Not a peep. You'd think he'd say something after not showing last night. You think he'll contact me again?"

"I don't know. He didn't get the money. If it's Roger, he's scared, but he needs cash. We'll have to wait and see what he does."

"I told my wife about the affair." His voice was heavy.

"Wow. But ... that's good, right? What did she say?"

"About what you might expect. She sure wasn't happy about it." He drew in a sad breath. "We have a lot of work if we're going to make our marriage work. I don't know where things will go. But maybe this whole thing has been good for me. It finally got things out in the open. I need to figure out some stuff."

"Yes, that's a good idea."

I reiterated he should call me with any news, ended the call, and contacted Dennis. "You talked to Michelle?"

"Yes. She's worried. I told her to hang tight for a while. She's not too happy with me."

That seemed a common family theme. "Did you tell her about the hit-and-run?"

"No, but I will. What're you doing today?"

"I'm going to see if I can find any evidence that Roger is the blackmailer."

"If he did that to me ..." He left the rest unsaid.

"Stay low and contact me if you hear from Roger, or anyone else in the family."

"Will do."

I pocketed my phone and tried to wear Humphrey out by having him chase a laser pointer until Willie was out of the shower. She and I ate a quick bowl of cereal. Then I got ready, packed a cooler with a sandwich and snacks, and headed out the door. I arrived at the Farley house before ten, and I parked down the street. I rolled down the window and waited. At eleven, Michelle and Roger left in her dark Escalade. They drove to the Denver Country Club, and I found an inconspicuous parking space across the street. The day dragged on, and I ate my sandwich. The Farleys were inside for several hours. I, on the other hand, sat in my car and read a David Baldacci thriller on my phone. They finally emerged from the country club around four, then drove to Elway's and had dinner. After that they went home.

On Sunday, other than a quick errand to the grocery store and running in the park, Roger stayed home. Cal and I talked. Other than the Imperial Supply financial mess, he hadn't found that Roger was involved in any other business endeavors.

On Monday, I was parked near the Farley house at six. The morning was pleasant, not hot yet, and I was wide awake. A little after seven, Roger's truck backed out of the garage and he drove off in the other direction. A few minutes later, Michelle left with Andy in the passenger seat. I followed her to Mowery Transportation, and she parked next to Roger's truck in front of the office. The lot was busy, people and trucks and trailers coming and going. I saw Isaac moving between the warehouses, talking to truckers, inspecting trucks. Ben was there as well, and he and Isaac talked several times. Roger joined them for a while, and he also walked around and looked at some of the rigs. Then he went back into the office.

"Eyes and ears of the company," I said to myself.

I continued to watch the lot. A little after eleven, Christie came out of the building, got in her car, and drove away. Some other employees left as well. At noon, Roger emerged and walked to his truck. He backed out and drove to the gate, then turned in my direction. I ducked down as he drove past me. I glanced in the side mirror. The truck turned right. I started the 4-Runner and quickly followed. Roger got onto I-70 and headed to the Five Points neighborhood, north of downtown. There was plenty of traffic, and I was able to keep distance between him and me. He soon parked in front of a rundown two-story office building. He got out and walked inside. I parked and hurried toward the entrance. No one was around as I peeked into the building. Roger had crossed the foyer and was headed down a hall to the right. I slipped inside the building and tiptoed toward the hall. I glanced around the corner. Roger was going into an office at the end. I ran back outside and around the building. I slowed as I neared the corner, then suddenly halted when – through a window – I saw Roger enter the corner office. A man with dark hair was sitting at a desk. I ducked behind a tree and watched. Traffic went by on the streets, but the parking lot was quiet. I was sure no one saw me.

Roger took a seat across from the man. I took a few quick pictures of them with my phone and kept watching. The man looked calm, but something about him seemed dangerous. Roger talked for a minute, and the man sat back. Roger ran out of steam, and the man shook his head and said something. Roger held up his hands. The man then pointed at him, and Roger frowned. The conversation continued, and then Roger stood up and gestured. The man didn't seem fazed, and he shrugged. Roger said something else and finally backed out of the room. I waited until the man looked down at his desk and then walked quickly back toward the building entrance and hid behind some tall bushes. None too soon. Roger stormed out of the building, his brow furrowed. He got in his truck and peeled out of the parking lot.

I was tempted to follow him, but I wanted to know more about what had just happened, so once the truck vanished into traffic, I walked back inside the building. I went down the hall and paused at the far door with a sign that read, "Frick and Associates." Very nondescript. I yanked out my phone and googled it, but found nothing. I tried the knob. The door opened, and I stepped into a small waiting area that smelled stale. A couple of chairs lined one wall, and an empty desk sat opposite. The walls were bare, and a computer and monitor on the desk were turned off. There was no phone. I heard a voice down the hall and I followed it past an empty office. I stopped near the corner office and glanced inside. The man I'd seen with Roger was on the phone.

"Yeah, I'll handle it." His voice was deep. He paused. "Don't worry about it. I'm sure he'll come up with it, and if he doesn't, I know how to take care of it. Like I said, you don't have to worry."

He grunted and talked a bit about the Rockies game, and then the phone slammed down. He swore, and it was quiet. He began writing something down. I stepped into the doorway and looked at him. He had a wide, swarthy face, dark hair, and big hands. What I could see of his upper body was thick, muscles bulging from his short-sleeved shirt. His arms were hairy, and hair protruded from the back of his neck as well. He was someone who could handle himself.

"No one was out front," I began.

If he was surprised, he didn't show it. "What can I do for you?"

I decided to be blunt. "I need some information about Roger Farley."

He set the pen down and looked at me. "I'm not sure who you mean."

I jerked a thumb down the hall. "He was just here. Meeting with you."

His eyes narrowed. "You're not a cop. I would know."

I shrugged. "No, I'm not." I glanced at the nondescript white walls, the lack of any personal touch. Just a baseball bat leaning in a corner. "What do you do here?"

He tipped his head as he contemplated me. "We buy and sell stuff, and help out people where we can."

It was vague, but I suddenly realized what he must be doing.

"You loaned money to Roger, didn't you?"

He put his meaty hands on the desk. "Who are you?"

I didn't want to tell him that. I didn't trust him any more than he trusted me. I've been known on occasion to use one of my favorite fictional detectives as an alias, and it seemed wise to do so now. "I'm Sam Spade," I said, borrowing the detective's name from Dashiell Hammett's novel, *The Maltese Falcon,* the character Humphrey Bogart made famous in the movie of the same name. "And you are?"

"Your worst nightmare, if you keep lying to me." He sat back, an amused smile on his face. "Humphrey Bogart, right?"

"You know your detectives," I said. "I'm not looking for any trouble, I only want to know what Roger Farley was doing here."

He gave that some consideration. Then he stood up to give me the full threat of his big frame. "Okay, I'll tell you what you want to know. I'm not scared of you."

I wasn't sure how to take that. Part of me was insulted that I might've come across as wimpy, but I also didn't want any trouble. And I remembered the bat in the corner. I shrugged and let him continue.

"Roger owes me a chunk of change. He was supposed to pay that off today, but he came up empty-handed." His face went dark. "I don't like it when somebody tells me they're going to bring me my money, and they don't. I let Roger know that."

"Why didn't he have the money?"

"He said he was supposed to get it last Friday, but he didn't. He asked for a few more days."

"And you agreed?"

An eyebrow shot up menacingly. "You saw him walk out of here, didn't you?"

I nodded. "Did he tell you how he's going to get the money?"

He shook his head. "No, and I don't care, just as long as he brings it to me."

"What happens if he doesn't? You break his legs?"

He held up a hand, as if threatening or hurting people was a common occurrence for him. "That's such a cliché. But, if I don't get my money ..."

I glanced around. "What if I were to tell the police about you?"

His face was stony. "You wouldn't want to do that."

On the one hand, it was an innocent comment. On the other, it held more threat than I'd probably heard from anybody in my entire life. I forced a smile.

"You don't have to worry about me. I'm here to resolve an issue for my client. Thank you."

He nodded, back to being entertained by me. "If you see Roger, tell him to get me my money. I don't care about you, your client, or anything else."

"Right."

I'd gotten what I wanted, and the baseball bat was still undisturbed in the corner, so I quietly walked down the hallway and left.

CHAPTER THIRTY

I stopped at a Wendy's for a quick burger, then used the restroom and drove back to Mowery Transportation. The whole time, my mind was on the man at Frick and Associates. It didn't take a genius to know you didn't mess with a man like that. Roger Farley had gotten himself into some big trouble. And he needed money. I debated whether to confront him immediately, but as I drove to Mowery Transportation, I decided not to. Not just yet. Roger would surely take the opportunity to lie to me, and to cover his tracks. I had still only circumstantial evidence against him, which wasn't good enough. But what to do? I ran through possible scenarios, and by the time I reached Mowery, I decided to talk to Michelle first. I wanted to know if she knew about Roger's business dealings, and if so, what she thought about all that. And if she had any inkling that her husband might be a blackmailer. She'd sounded worried the last time I'd talked to her. However, when I parked at Mowery, I didn't see her car out front. I went inside, anyway. Christie looked up at me, and fear leapt into her eyes.

"Can I help you?" Her voice shook. I'm sure she thought I was going to confront her about her affair with Ben. Instead, I threw her a curveball.

"Is Michelle here?" I asked, even though I thought I knew the answer.

She shook her head. "No, she's gone for the afternoon. Would you like me to have her call you if she checks in?"

I held up a hand. "No, I'll catch up with her myself. I have her number."

I turned to leave, and I heard an audible sigh of relief from her. Then I turned back to her, and she held her breath.

"The other night," I said. "Did you see anything when you left?"

She didn't bother denying anything. "I didn't see you, if that's what you mean."

"Anyone else?"

She thought for a moment. "Roger left later that night. A little before ... me."

"You saw him?"

Another headshake. "No. His truck." She turned red. "I should've known he'd be around."

I didn't reply to that. "Thanks."

She seemed relieved, and I left the office. I called Michelle, but she didn't answer. I sat in my car for a moment, thinking. Then I texted Willie that I didn't know when I would be home, but that I thought I was close to resolving things. She was at work today, and I didn't hear back. I started the 4-Runner and pulled out of the lot.

I ran a couple of errands and went back by the condo to check on Humphrey. Michelle never called back. At four o'clock, I was back in the Farleys' neighborhood. I parked down the street from their house and waited. It was another hot afternoon, and I rolled down the window and listened to the Psychedelic Furs, the volume low. Willie texted back and wished me luck, and when I looked up, Michelle's Escalade was pulling into her garage. Roger's truck wasn't there.

Showtime, I thought to myself. I waited until the garage door shut, got out, and hurried to the front door. I rang the bell. Low chimes sounded within. I wanted to catch Michelle by surprise, not give her time to think or relax. A moment later, the front door opened and she looked at me. She looked tired, dark circles under her eyes.

"Reed. I wasn't expecting you." She peered through the screen at me.

"I called."

"It's been a busy afternoon. Sorry."

"Do you have a moment?" I asked.

She frowned and dabbed at the corner of an eye, careful not to smudge her makeup. "I just got home from work."

"I see," I said, even though I knew that. I gave her a firm look. "It's important."

Her jaw worked as she seemed to search for an excuse, then she opened the screen door and stepped back. "Come on in."

I entered the wide marble-tiled foyer, and she led me around the corner to a living room with plush white carpet, off-white couches, and white walls. The paintings on the walls were pastels, matted and framed in white. I always felt as if I were in a snowstorm when I entered one of these all-white homes. She took a seat at a couch under the window, and I perched on a white wingback chair. I looked past her, out a big bay window. I could see the driveway and the street. A few kids rode by on bicycles, then it was quiet. I heard water running upstairs and wondered if Jordan and Andy were home.

Michelle smoothed a hand over her tan slacks and stared at me. "What's going on?"

I studied her carefully. Did she know anything about what Roger was up to? I couldn't tell.

"As you know, I've been doing a lot of running around," I said. I paused, and she waited expectantly. "It's been rather difficult trying to track down the blackmailer when the incident occurred over a year ago."

Another dab at her eyes. "Yes, I know. Dennis said you've been having trouble with your investigation. Does this mean you're giving up?"

An interesting turn in the conversation. I shook my head.

"No, I've actually found out something different. It turns out, the blackmailer is active again."

She opened her mouth in surprise. "Really? Who is it?"

I was cautious. "I'm not going to reveal who just yet, but knowing there's another victim led me in a whole different direction."

She sat up straighter. "Someone at Mowery is being blackmailed again?" She swore softly. "If I get my hands on that person ..."

Be careful what you wish for, I thought to myself. I watched her for a moment. The house was silent. She didn't seem as if she were hiding anything, no darting her eyes away from me, no nervousness. I went on.

"I've done a lot of research on a lot of different people, and at first, I was thinking maybe Clyde Hessler was guilty."

She shook her head vehemently. "I told you it's not Clyde. It can't be."

I stared at her. "Well, I wasn't so sure about that. Clyde has some big sums of money that it would seem he can't account for. At least I can't account for that."

"Maybe he gambles," she said, almost as if she knew that might be the case.

I shrugged. "Yes, that could be true. But as I looked at things more, I came across another person of interest."

"Who?" She shifted in her seat, suddenly agitated. "Don't keep me in suspense."

I fished for information. "Let me ask you this. How much do you and your husband talk about your finances? Do you share them, know what each other does, where the money goes?"

She put a hand on the couch and smoothed the fabric. "What do you mean? You think Roger ..." She couldn't finish.

"I started scrutinizing everyone who works at Mowery. I didn't think anything about Roger at first, but then some things didn't quite make sense."

Her gaze strayed to the hallway for a moment. "What?"

"First, he hasn't been particularly complementary of his in-laws, especially Dennis."

"I know Roger doesn't like Dennis," she said quickly.

"Did you know that Roger doesn't like working at Mowery Transportation, either, that he —"

"Oh, everyone knows that," she interrupted with a scowl. "Even I do. Roger always said he wanted to start his own business, but here's the thing." She jabbed a finger at me. "He's a terrible businessman. When we were dating, he was working for his own father, and his father even told me that. He said of all things, watch your money because Roger isn't good with it." She stared at the floor sadly. "I know it sounds terrible to say that, but it's true. Roger thinks much more highly of his own skills than anybody else does. He's lucky he got a job at Mowery, lucky that my dad put up with him all these years."

"That's an interesting take," I said. "Does Ben know this?"

She shook her head. "Dad was helping out, but we didn't tell anyone else about Roger." Her head jerked up. "Did Roger talk to you? What did you hear?"

"I hadn't heard about his being bad with money, just that he's unhappy. But one thing a couple of people have confirmed is that Roger is the eyes and ears of the company. If anything was going on around Mowery, Roger would know it."

She stared at me. "So what? You're saying that Roger knew about Dennis's skimming? How? Did Roger look at the books himself?" She coughed uncomfortably. "I don't want to disparage my own husband, but frankly, I don't see how he'd know enough to catch things like that."

"Maybe not, but he could've overheard Dennis telling somebody else, and then used that to his advantage."

"But blackmail Dennis? I don't believe it." Her tone was firm.

"I realize this is circumstantial, but hear me out." I went on. "Roger's also in financial trouble. That's why I wanted to know what you knew."

She shifted again, becoming even more agitated. "That can't be. I handle our finances."

"Did you know he started a company about sixteen months ago, around the time that Dennis was being blackmailed? From what I could find, the company lost money. Maybe Roger needed some quick cash to get himself out of a bind."

She flicked a hand at me. "Impossible. I'm sure I would've found out."

"Just like you would've found out that Dennis was skimming?" I pointed out.

She didn't protest. "Okay, maybe I missed that."

"Roger is in another business deal now. He started a company called Imperial Supply."

"I don't know anything about Imperial." She was talking fast now, angry.

"And he's in some financial trouble again."

Her voice was tight. "How do you know this?"

I shrugged. "I have my ways. The company is in trouble, and he owes some bad people some money. If he doesn't pay them back soon, he'll be in some serious danger."

She stared at me uneasily. "I don't believe it."

From the hall came a voice. "I don't, either."

We both turned. Roger was standing in the doorway. I hadn't heard him come in, didn't even realize he was home. It must've been him running water upstairs.

I stared at him, not backing down. "It's true," I said. "I followed you today and saw you talking with that goon at Frisk and Associates."

Roger's eyes were angry slits. "You should mind your own business."

I held up my hands. "I was hired to find a blackmailer." I gestured at him. "You."

He swore at me. "I may be in some trouble with this new business, but I'm not a blackmailer." He turned to Michelle, muscles tense. "You have to believe me. I was trying to make a go of this company, trying to show you that I can do things, too. I know how to handle a business."

She gasped. "Really? Then how come you're in so deep you're borrowing money from a loan shark?" She almost sobbed. "What kind of trouble have you gotten yourself into? Why can't it be enough that you just work at Mowery?"

He snorted. "Because I don't want to be everyone's lackey, going around, just watching things. Your father and uncle have never trusted me to really handle anything."

"Can you blame them?" she asked. "And you blackmailed Dennis?"

"I'm telling you I didn't."

I turned to Michelle. "You told Roger about hiring me, and you gave him updates?" She nodded. I looked at Roger. "You know everything that's going on, and when I was hired, you panicked. You couldn't show up at the blackmail drop the other night, either, because you knew you might get caught. But that meant you didn't have the money for the loan shark."

He stared at me. "Why do you think that?"

I laid out my case. "The blackmailer had to be somebody at the company, or somebody that knew what Dennis was doing. That meant a lot of people. Then I found out Dennis thought somebody may have overheard him talking on the phone about his skimming activities. What's more, someone else is being blackmailed now. And the blackmailer has to be somebody who's the eyes and ears of the company, somebody who knows what's going on." I pointed at him. "Everyone says that about you. You're all over the place, keeping tabs on what happens at Mowery. People have seen your truck around, too." Something else occurred to me. "You're about the height of the blackmailer, and thin like he was."

"That could be anybody," Michelle protested.

"I never overheard Dennis saying anything," Roger said.

"What about a Monday night over a year ago?" I asked. "The Broncos played the Bears, and Dennis was at the office, drunk. So drunk that he was telling a friend what he was doing, and he thought he overheard somebody listening to him."

Michelle let out a relieved but humorless laugh. "That couldn't have been Roger. He and I take a dance class every Monday night. Every fall, from September until Thanksgiving."

"Yeah, which means I miss Monday night games," Roger said, his voice irritated. He looked at me, almost embarrassed. "I agreed to the class because she said she'd go on fishing trips with me."

"Talk about boring," Michelle said. "But we compromised for each other."

As Michelle talked, I saw movement out the window behind her. Roger's black truck pulled quickly into the driveway and jerked to a stop. Pieces of the puzzle swirled in my head. Roger had come home with Michelle. Someone else drove his truck home. A lanky figure in a dark hoodie got out. He turned and I saw who it was.

Andy Farley.

Then I realized how I'd been looking at things all wrong.

CHAPTER THIRTY-ONE

I stared out the window.
"What?" Roger said, his voice irritated. He peered out the window as well. "Andy borrowed my truck today."
I nodded slowly. "Someone else is the eyes and ears of the company, too," I said quietly.
Michelle twisted on the couch and looked out the window. Andy was headed up the walk. She turned to me.
"Andy? You can't be serious."
"Someone saw your truck around the company," I said to Roger. "Only it wasn't you, was it? Someone is learning the ropes at Mowery Transportation, which gives him a reason to be around the property a lot."
The front door opened and shut, and Andy walked down the hall and into the doorway. He looked at his dad, then his mom.
"What?" he asked, sounding much like his father.
Standing next to Roger, I noticed that Andy was about the same build, but slightly smaller. He easily fit the description of the man that Taylor Walsh had seen in the alley behind Billy's, the description he'd given to Ace and Deuce. Andy realized everyone was staring at him, and he bit his lip. Then he repeated, "What?"

My mind raced. Everything I'd thought about Roger, all my assumptions about his involvement in blackmailing Dennis and Ben, could fit for Andy.

"Where were you last Thursday night?" I asked him.

"Last Thursday? Uh, I was out with friends," he said. His voice was soft, tinged with nervousness.

"Roger," I said. "Does your truck have GPS?"

He nodded. "Yes, it does."

I stared at Andy. "You know, technology is so great these days that if I wanted to, I could pinpoint exactly where the truck was that night."

Andy tried to keep eye contact, but he couldn't. He looked away.

"Andy," Michelle said. "What do you know about your uncle's blackmail? Did you do that to Dennis?"

Andy took a step away from his dad and shook his head. "Mom, I don't know what you're talking about."

Roger whirled on him. "You better tell us what's going on right now! That guy," he jabbed a finger at me, "thinks I had something to do with blackmailing Dennis."

Andy gulped. He shifted from foot to foot, seemed to realize he was trapped, and he spoke in a small voice.

"It's not what you think. I didn't mean any real harm."

Michelle jumped to her feet. "Are you kidding me? You blackmailed your uncle?"

I wanted to say "and his great-uncle," but I held back.

Andy gnawed his lip, then suddenly found some courage – or arrogance. "Dennis got what he deserved. You said it. He stole from the company and he shouldn't have."

She stared at him, stunned. "I didn't mean he should be *blackmailed*. How did you know?"

Andy shrugged. "It was during the school year while I worked there part-time. I was doing my homework at lunch, and I forgot one of my textbooks. I went back that night to get it. Dennis was there, and he was drunk." His tone was laced with derision. "I overheard him talking to someone, and he was going on about how he was skimming off the company books. I left after I heard that, and he didn't know it was me."

Roger stared at him. "Why didn't you tell us about it?"

Andy sneered. "What would you do? Nothing. And I needed the money."

"What for?" Michelle was incredulous. "Are you in some kind of trouble? Gambling?"

Andy let out an uneasy laugh. "Of course not. I was saving up money so I could leave." He gaped at his parents. "I know what you guys want to do. It's a family business, and you want me to work there. I told you I didn't want to do that. I want to go to Europe." He glared at them. "But neither one of you believe me." He gave his dad a scathing look. "You tell me I can do my own thing, but I know you, you'll just have me working at the company just like you. Well, I don't want that. When I heard Dennis, I saw an opportunity and I took it."

"How did you know Taylor Walsh?" I asked.

He shrugged. "He used to be in college, and he still knows people. Everybody knows he deals drugs, and that he can keep his mouth shut. I figured if I offered him enough money, he'd help out. And he did. He was the perfect go-between."

"You never thought you might get caught?" Roger asked.

"No," Andy said.

Michelle moved toward him. "Reed said someone else is being blackmailed. Who?"

Andy didn't have the discretion that I did. "Uncle Ben. He's having an affair with Christie."

Michelle gasped, and Roger's jaw dropped.

"I don't believe it," Michelle finally said.

Andy's look was dangerous. "It's true. You can ask him."

She narrowed her eyes at him. "You're blackmailing him, too?"

Andy shrugged. "If he was going to be that stupid, yes."

Andy was scary. He obviously had no feelings for his relatives. Michelle and Roger were stunned speechless. They were seeing their son in a whole different light. It was sad. Sometimes the people who you think are the least likely to do something are the ones most likely to do it. What a family. What a mess.

"You beat up Dennis?" Michelle asked.

Now Andy protested. "No. I just wanted to scare him, so I hired someone. He was supposed to scare Dennis. I wanted Dennis to fire this guy," he said pointedly at me. "But the guy I hired got carried away and beat up Dennis."

"Your uncle." Roger shook his head, incredulous. "I can't believe you'd do that."

"You don't like him," Andy said dully.

"Yeah, but I wouldn't do that!" Roger snapped.

Something occurred to me. "Were you following me the other night?" I asked Andy. "Were you watching the park, where the blackmail drop was supposed to happen?"

He nodded. "I've been trying to figure out what you knew. I didn't want to get caught." He sighed, then looked at his parents, his tone neutral. "Are you going to call the police?"

Neither Roger nor Michelle said anything for a moment. Then she gestured at the couch. "Andy, sit down."

He glanced at me as if I could help. I didn't do a thing. He hesitated, then moved slowly into the room, a look of defiance on his face. He didn't seem to be sorry for anything. A budding sociopath?

Michelle turned to me. "Reed, we need some private time. May I call you tomorrow?"

I nodded and stood up. "I'm sorry things turned out the way they did."

She could barely find her voice. "Me, too."

She stared at Andy. Roger gestured for me to follow him, and he let me out. I heard him swearing as the door shut.

The next few days were a blur. Michelle called me. She said that she and Roger were dealing with Andy, that he was going to pay back all the blackmail money, and they were getting him into counseling. She asked for my address to pay me my final check. As she talked, she sounded so down, so dejected. Her world had been shattered, in more ways than one. I met Dennis the next afternoon at the Starbucks for coffee. He looked tired, and his face was still bruised.

"What're you going to do now?" I asked as we sipped coffee.

He shrugged. "You may not believe me, but I really didn't know what I was going to do if you found the blackmailer. Now that I know it's Andy, I feel incredibly sad. He's going down the wrong path, and I hope he can get some help. He was always kind of cool toward me, but I never would've thought he could stoop so low."

"He did an awful thing."

He stared at the mall and sighed. "You asked so many questions about my family and me, and I hesitated to share too much. There's a lot in creating a successful company, but it puts pressure on everyone." He thought for a moment. "Michelle has too much pride about the company, doesn't she?"

"Possibly."

"I was afraid if I told you that's how I felt, you'd tell Michelle. Isaac always said Michelle pushed him too hard."

I sipped coffee and studied him. "What're you going to do about the hit-and-run?"

He stared at the table for a moment. "It's not easy for me to say this, but you're right. I'm not going to stay sober if I can't be honest about everything. I went to the police this morning and told them about the accident. Thankfully, the man I hit is okay. They're going to press charges, but since the guy I hit wasn't hurt, it will be a misdemeanor. I suppose that guy could sue me, not sure for what, but again, since he wasn't hurt, that likely won't happen. I'm going to talk to him, if he'll see me. I want to apologize personally. I already feel better, though. And I'm so relieved that man was okay, for his sake and for my own."

I smiled. "That's good to hear. You won't regret the decision."

We sat for a minute and finished our coffee, and then he glanced at his phone. "I need to go now. Thanks for all your help. Our family has a lot to deal with, but it's good that this is all being resolved, or at least, we're making a start at it."

I waved at him as he got up and walked away. I sat for a minute, thinking about his situation, and I was reminded again of the film *In A*

Lonely Place. However, unlike Bogie's Dixon Steele character, Dennis seemed to be turning a corner, maybe even escaping his demons. I hoped so. But my heart was still heavy. I threw out my cup and went home.

Later that day, Willie and I were sitting in Doctor Rivera's office. He was talking, and I had to focus on what he was saying. Willie had gotten the diagnostic mammogram, and rather than hearing that all was okay, the doctor had requested a visit. Now, when he uttered the words "cancer," the world seemed to stop. I held Willie's hand hard. She focused on him.

"We need to get some more information," Doctor Rivera said, "so I want you to get a biopsy to determine the type of cancer. We'll see what the results are, but I want you to be prepared. I also want you to remember, based on what I'm seeing, the prognosis is good. This type of cancer is very treatable, very survivable, with the right treatment."

"Okay," Willie said, her voice soft. I knew she was stunned, and so was I.

Doctor Rivera stood up. "I'll have you contact a surgeon as well. Then we'll wait for the PET scan results and go from there."

Willie and I stood up, and he put a hand on her shoulder. "We're going to take very, very good care of you."

She and I thanked him, and we walked out of the office. We rode an elevator to the lobby in silence and walked outside.

"We have to take this one day at a time," I said.

"Yes," she replied.

She didn't say a word as we went to my car and got in. I didn't start it, and we sat in silence for a minute.

"I don't know what to think," she said.

"I don't, either."

Before I could say more, my phone rang, and I looked at it and sighed. "It's Mom."

Willie sighed and nodded. "You might as well answer it."

"Should I tell her?"

She didn't reply.

I answered. "Reed, dear, it's your mother." As if I didn't know. "I won't take up too much of your time, but honey, I'm worried. You didn't sound like yourself the other day, and your father and I have been worried since then. Is something going on?"

I glanced at Willie, and she nodded.

"Willie's with me, Mom." I put the phone on speaker.

"Oh, Willie, honey, how are you.?"

"I suppose not too well at the moment," Willie said.

"What's wrong?" Mom asked.

Willie drew in a breath and then told her about the diagnostic mammogram results. My mother gasped, and when she spoke, she sounded on the verge of tears.

"Honey, I'm so sorry to hear that." She said more, but I didn't really hear it. "Let's take it day by day. And remember, if the doctors say that the prognosis is good, then we have to hold onto that and pray for the best. You know that we love you."

Willie smiled. "Yes, I do."

"Reed, your father and I are here for both of you. We're your family, and we'll do anything for you."

I reached over and held Willie's hand. "Yes, Mom, I know you're here for us." That was the best we had at the moment.

AUTHOR'S NOTE

Dear Reader,

If you enjoyed *In a Lowly Place*, would you please write an honest review? You have no idea how much it warms my heart to get a new review. And this isn't just for me. Think of all the people out there who need reviews to make decisions, and you would be helping them.

You are awesome for doing so, and I am grateful to you!

ABOUT THE AUTHOR

Renée's early career as a counselor gives her a unique ability to write characters with depth and personality, and she now works as a business analyst. She lives in the mountains west of Denver, Colorado and enjoys hiking, cycling, and reading when she's not busy writing her next novel.

Renée loves to travel and has visited numerous countries around the world. She has also spent many summer days at her parents' cabin in the hills outside of Boulder, Colorado, which was the inspiration for the setting of Taylor Crossing in her novel *Nephilim*.

She is the author of the Reed Ferguson mysteries, the Dewey Webb historical mysteries, and the Sarah Spillman police procedurals. She also wrote the standalone suspense novels *The Girl in the Window* and *What's Yours is Mine*, *Nephilim: Genesis of Evil*, a supernatural thriller, along with children's novels and other short stories.

Visit Renée at www.reneepawlish.com.

RENÉE'S BOOKSHELF

The Sarah Spillman Mysteries:

Deadly Connections

Deadly Invasion

Deadly Guild

Deadly Revenge

Deadly Judgment

Deadly Target

Deadly Corruption

Deadly Past

Deadly Christmas

Seven for Suicide

Saturday Night Special

Dance of the Macabre

Detective Sarah Spillman Mystery Series Boxsets

Sarah Spillman Mysteries Books 1 - 3

Standalone Psychological Suspense:

The Girl in the Window

What's Yours Is Mine

Reed Ferguson Mysteries:

This Doesn't Happen In The Movies

Reel Estate Rip-Off

The Maltese Felon

Farewell, My Deuce

Out Of The Past

Torch Scene
✓ The Lady Who Sang High
Sweet Smell Of Sucrets
The Third Fan
Back Story
Night of the Hunted
The Postman Always Brings Dice
Road Blocked
Small Town Focus
Nightmare Sally
The Damned Don't Die
Double Iniquity
The Lady Rambles
A Killing
Dangers on a Train
✓ In a Lowly Place
Ace in the Hole
Walk Softly, Danger
Elvis And The Sports Card Cheat
A Gun For Hire
Cool Alibi
The Big Steal
The Wrong Woman

Dewey Webb Historical Mystery Series:

Web of Deceit
Murder In Fashion
Secrets and Lies
Honor Among Thieves
Trouble Finds Her

Mob Rule

Murder At Eight

Second Chance

Double Cross

The Noah Winter Adventure
(A Young Adult Mystery Series)

The Emerald Quest

Dive into Danger

Terror On Lake Huron

Take Five Collection (Mystery Anthology)

Nephilim Genesis of Evil (Supernatural Mystery)

Codename Richard: A Ghost Story

The Taste of Blood: A Vampire Story

This War We're In (Middle-grade Historical Fiction)

Nonfiction:

The Sallie House: Exposing the Beast Within

Made in the USA
Middletown, DE
06 July 2023